Casualty Loss

Casualty Loss

Jim Weikart

Walker and Company
New York

Copyright © 1991 by Jim Weikart

All the characters and events portrayed in this work are fictitious.

First published in the United States of America in 1991
by Walker Publishing Company, Inc.
Published simultaneously in Canada by Thomas Allen & Son
Canada, Limited, Markham, Ontario

Library of Congress Cataloging-in-Publication Data

Weikart, Jim
Casualty loss / Jim Weikart.
p.   cm.
ISBN 0-8027-5790-1
I. Title.
PS3573.E38369C3   1991
813'.54—dc20   91-2644
CIP

Printed in the United States of America
2 4 6 8 10 9 7 5 3 1

In Memory of
William A. Owens

Special thanks to:

Estate attorney Josh Rubenstein and Sergeant Richard Sealander of the Connecticut State Police for information provided.

Also to Robert Anderson, Esther Cohen, Janet Hutchings, Edite Kroll, Elizabeth Servideo, and Lynne.

Casualty Loss

$\triangledown$

Chapter 1

THE FILMING WENT WELL.

Not that I was much help. Anne handled thirteen characters—ten adults and three children—for a film about us she was making for her M.F.A. thesis. She wanted us to be ourselves and especially for Donald, Joan, and Elaine to tell the stories they always did, but this time concentrating on the best of the year—or the decade for that matter. The ultimate dinner party.

Anne and I lived together in the city. My brother, Donald, lived summers in a big country house with his wife, Joan, and two single men, Frederik and Clark. It was a communal deal. The house, built in 1812, had been part of the underground railway.

Elaine always came to their dinners with her husband, Nick. They were also members of this group modeled after the communes of the sixties but relegated now to country weekends isolated from real lives in the city. Frank Murphy—called Murph—the local postmaster and Nancy, his wife, were relative newcomers (Anne had needed someone to be the audience). Anne and I, of course, were part of this sixties grouping as an extension of Donald and Joan, as were the kids—Donald and Joan's two-year-old Dillon and six-year-old Jennifer. And Elaine and Nick's four-year-old Josh.

1

It was the day after Christmas and although this kind of
dinner party was more reminiscent of the warm, slow days
of August, we all agreed to participate for Anne's sake. She
had conceived of the film as a project for her thesis for NYU
film school. She wanted the children excluded, but Joan said
no, the children were as much a part of these dinners as the
adults and no record of one of them would be complete without them. So they were there too, making demands and some
noise throughout. Light snow drifted past the windows, and
the fires had been laid in all the main fireplaces.

Anne did a good job of preparing for the filming, having
researched everything from Bergman's Christmas dinner in
Fanny and Alexander to *Annie Hall*, *Babette's Feast*, and all
the *Godfather* dinners. She felt her cameras and lights were
just fine. Everyone pitched in to cook a good meal, and at
Anne's direction we all "arrived" at the door and stamped
the snow off our feet, hung up our coats and capes, and were
ushered in to the table.

The meal was delicious. Roast beef, Yorkshire pudding,
and a good Bordelaise sauce served on mashed potatoes or
acorn squash. The wine was a very nice Chateauneuf-du-
Pape, and Anne insisted there be plenty of it to keep things
rolling smoothly. All the service was silver and the place
settings were Wedgwood blue. A Waldorf salad made from
apples from the orchard was set on a bed of red-leaf lettuce
at every place setting except for those of the two youngest
children. Anne had banned candles because she worried
about the additional lighting problems. After dinner there
were apple and pumpkin pies, whipped cream, and coffee.

And drugs. They still had that from the sixties too. Donald had an old moroccon leather box that he called his
Pandora's Choice and inside he kept things to snort, eat, or
smoke that society officially condemns. Donald led the argument for adult freedom of choice. I opposed him.

As usual, Joan and Elaine kept things going. They both
looked good. Joan had curly brown hair and wore dangling
blue earrings. She had on a long white cotton gown with a
white lace collar. At just over five feet, she was the shortest

of the adults there. Anne had asked her not to describe people as "all fucked up" during the film, particularly not people she knew.

Anne counted on Elaine to carry the most positive beat. Elaine was both a painter and a poet. For the dinner, she wore unmatched earrings—one a black onyx surrounded by tiny marcasites and the other a gold filigree. Her dress was a long, flowing black velvet with a deep open neckline more than hinting at a fine cleavage. Elaine's red hair and dominant voice made her the mistress of ceremonies anywhere. She had sharp brown eyes and a way of questioning that could bring anyone out. She would have been the best psychologist of any of us, but Joan made her living that way, not Elaine.

Donald, the third of the key trio for Anne's film, wore a brilliant red silk shirt open at the collar, which set off his single diamond ear stud. His head was bald except for a monk's fringe of hair above the ears.

Of the group, only Frederik seemed reticent. He had shown up but wore only a plain white T-shirt and Levi's and said nothing much throughout the dinner, just sitting back observing us with his dark eyes. He had black hair down to the nape and a full black beard with a thread or two of gray. The T-shirt was his way of protesting the filming. Even though Frederik, like Donald, made a good living editing films, he saw Anne as intruding into our private lives with her project.

Anne had shot a few frames of us all arriving and having drinks but the primary take opened in the dining room as we gathered around the table. Donald sat at the head of the table and little Dillon was at his left, then Joan, Murph and Nan, and finally me. On the other side, Elaine took the first seat with her child Josh beside her and then six-year-old Jennifer, Nick, and Frederik. Anne sat next to Frederik where she could most easily be up from her chair to work with her three person film crew. Clark sat at the foot of the table opposite Donald—the end nearest the kitchen—because he would be up and down serving the meal.

As Donald dipped forward to sit down, I could just make out the small scar on the top of his head where a nightstick had caught him during the Chicago Days of Rage. Donald, running in the front of a tear-gassed demonstration, reached a place where the cop were crouched behind parked trucks waiting, when one jumped out to catch him with a hard cheap shot on top of his head. Donald woke up in the hospital the next day. I was an eleven-year-old kid, still at home in Ohio at the time.

"Good food, good meat, good Lord, let's eat," Murph said in a mock grace and everyone except Nan laughed. Murph and Nan were Catholics. And it was the kind of thing that signaled to the rest of us that Murph might already have had too many drinks. Not only that he said it, but also because Nan didn't laugh with him.

But Anne kept filming. Clark began to carve the platter of roast beef. But, at over six feet and 260 pounds, Clark wielded the carving knife and fork like toys. Long brown hair hung down his back in a ponytail.

"This looks great," Elaine said, her brown eyes sparkling at the sight of all the food. She began to dish some potatoes onto Josh's plate. Donald did the same with green beans for Dillon, to which Dillon said, "Yucky!"

"I went to see Mr. Dorton today," Elaine said. "You know he runs a bookstore out of his living room. He calls it the Hopeful Berkshire. The thing about him is that he always sleeps with his tie on so that he'll be ready to greet guests." She held up her arms to show her bracelets and rings. "I'm wearing a million bracelets and a hundred rings. And I must go over there about every other week. But every time Mr. Dorton asks me, 'You new around here?'."

Everyone laughed on cue, and the conversation shifted to other topics. Joan launched into her theory of why Sigmund Freud hated women. Then at a signal from Anne, Murph picked up on the script—such as it was—which she had primed him and Nan for.

"How was it the likes of all of you got together?" he asked. "I mean I'm here frequently enough for dinner, but I've never heard the actual story of it all. It must be a lovely tale to hear."

"Cut," Anne shouted. Then she asked Murph where he got the sudden lilt in his speech. She requested that he speak with his normal voice, which might have an Irish cadence to it here and there but had no pronounced brogue. Murph agreed to try to do it right.

The take began with Murphy again asking the question.

"How was it this group of people got together? I've been here now quite a number of times for libations and food and I have yet to hear the story."

"Well, it's long and complicated," Joan said, turning to Murph beside her. They exchanged a peculiarly intense look. "I think Donald tells it best."

Strangely, Elaine was silent. I looked at little Dillon, who was looking up at his dad, and then at Donald himself. He smiled reflectively.

"Where should I start?" he said.

"In Vermont," Elaine said. "You should tell about the night you died."

"No," Nick said, "you have to give us the theory of twenty first." Nick's shoulder-length white hair and the crazy gleam in his blue eyes made him a colorful figure anywhere. He was a Vietnam vet.

Donald stood up and rapped on the table. "Listen up, everybody," he said. "Originally man lived like the great apes in small groups that totaled no more than twenty individuals. He related to this size group and gave large amounts of his time to interaction with everyone in it. They all knew each other well and gave support to everyone else in the group.

"In New York City, we meet many people who are attractive possibilities for our group of twenty. We become confused and try to include one hundred or two hundred people in the twenty. What happens is that we end up with no group at all—just a series of acquaintances we try to see as our friends. But they never get beyond being acquaintances— distant personalities who can never offer support and who we don't know how to aid and can't because there are too many of them.

"Even in New York City, one should form a group of twenty. Essentially, ten core members make up the group and ten more are in flux moving in or out. With a group of twenty, each of us knows he or she can creatively support each of the others and feel love and support in return. I believe it's more important than the family unit.

"You know I advocate making a list of your group of twenty. Especially for New York City. To prevent confusion and to focus the energy that has to be put into interaction."

Donald looked around at us. "My group of twenty includes all the people around this table." He spread his arms out like a priest giving a benediction. "I love you all," he said. "And I'd give you anything."

"Give us the story about Vermont," Elaine said again.

Donald bit his lower lip and looked around the table at us again. He led the biggest life of anyone I'd ever known. We always sat like disciples listening to his theories and stories, even though we'd all have denied that.

He looked down at Dillon and at Josh and Jennifer, who seemed to have finished eating. "You kids want to watch a video?" he asked. Dillon and Josh ran off to do that, but Jennifer sat right where she was, claiming she wanted to hear Dad tell his story again.

"All right," Donald said, "let's pick up on life in Vermont. It was the summer of 1975. I'd been living in a commune called the Maple Tree Farm in northern Vermont for a couple of years. Joan lived there. Clark lived there. Frederik lived there. And Elaine." Donald gestured affectionately toward each of them as he said the names.

"Except in the summer of 1975, Frederik had hitched out to Taos. And Elaine was over in Johnson at an art colony. So that left Joan and Clark with me. It got to be August and the wheat had been harvested and the orchards were just beginning to come into picking time. The vegetables and corn were brought in to keep our roadside stand going. I think there were fourteen adults and six children on the commune, keeping the place running. Five of the adults were just there for the summer.

"One night at dinner two new guests turned up. We frequently had guests come through. We had a rule somebody had to know them. And in fact it was Frederik in Taos that had sent these guests to us. They came together, arriving on a hot day in a cloud of dust pulling up in an old U.S. army surplus Jeep—an Indian named Painted River and his assistant, a young American who had adopted an Indian name, Snow Man. It was just before dinner and the whole crowd of us were sitting out behind the house as we often did that summer. We watched them come to a stop. Snow Man, the driver, got out of the Jeep first. He looked very striking because he was made up in Cherokee war paint. At least he called it Cherokee war paint. White stripes across the eyes and cheeks over a red ocher base. Then Painted River stepped down from the opposite side, maybe near sixty-five in age and so obviously very calm that he inspired spiritual confidence on contact.

" 'Hello,' this Snow Man said as they approached us together. 'Frederik said we would be welcome here.'

"So we set places for them at the table. As we ate, the Indian said he was trained in the ways of the traditional shaman. He called the new communes fertile grounds for teaching about the old ways. Snow Man said nothing but seemed to quietly affirm everything the old Indian said. If you want to get a sense of what was happening, imagine that you were someone in ancient Rome waiting for a visitation, and one of Christ's disciples had just come to dinner. That is how powerful Painted River's presence was to us. He was a man with a vision to show us. We were searching people in revolt against the prevailing system. Painted River looked around the table and asked if we wanted to train for a vision quest. Maybe this was the challenge we were waiting for, the event that would move us all into another kind of life. A vision of self at one with the planet and the universe. How can I describe for you the spiritual presence of this man? Our little band of atheists and agnostics was ready to follow him into battle. Can you believe it?"

At this point, little Dillon came running out from the

parlor, where the video was set up, and reached up to Donald to be picked up. Donald scooped him up and sat down in his chair. Dillon looked around the table and sat quietly. As Donald continued, he absentmindedly stroked Dillon's hair.

"Painted River and Snow Man went out to their tent shortly after dinner without getting an answer from any one of us or from us collectively—which was the way decisions were made at that time. We were up late into the night smoking some grass, talking about the vegetables and the children and whether we could spare anyone to go on a vision quest.

"At about one o'clock in the morning—very late for a farm—we decided that three of us could be spared to go. We drew straws, and they went to Joan and to Clark and to me. I went out to the tent. The flap was open and Painted River sat there waiting.

" 'Three of us wish to go on a vision quest.'

"Painted River said only one word—'good'—and then turned and closed the flap to his tent."

Donald paused and looked around the table. Nan was cutting the apple pie. "Send a big piece of that down here for Dillon and me to share," he said. Then he went on with the story.

"The next morning the Jeep, the tent, and all their stuff was gone. We didn't know why, but they seemed to have moved on. We spent most of the afternoon that day harvesting sweet corn under a clear, hot sky, coming home covered with sweat and the dry remains of corn silk all over us. When we came in sight of the house, we saw that the Jeep was back and Painted River stood beside it with Snow Man, in war paint as always, sitting on the ground behind him.

"They greeted us as we came up and Snow Man asked for the three who were coming on the vision quest. I raised my hand and pointed out Joan and Clark.

" 'Fine,' Painted River said. 'After dinner we start.'

"We all ate dinner that night with a sense of anticipation, even those who had to stay behind. Painted River talked about how hard it was to keep the Jeep mechanically fit and asked about our farming methods and compared them with the methods of Navajo Indians in the Southwest. Snow Man said nothing.

"After dinner the three of us brought our sleeping bags and climbed into the Jeep with Painted River and Snow Man, waving goodbye to the rest of the commune.

"Snow Man had driven us about twenty miles when he turned off onto an old logging road and shifted into four-wheel drive. We passed through a small woods, which screened us from the road, and he came to a stop along the eastern side of the woods under some large oak trees. Their tent was already pitched and we pitched our tent alongside, getting instruction from Snow Man to place it so that it would be shaded from the morning sun, as we would be sleeping into the days.

"Then Painted River emerged from his tent and indicated that we should follow him. So we went single file behind him—Joan, Clark, and me—with Snow Man bringing up the rear. He led us across the open field to a cut in the woods, and I could see that somebody had taken time to cut a usable pathway to the top of the hill. When we came out of the woods, there was a clear crest that rose above the trees so that the horizon was unobscured. A fire had been set in the middle of a circle, and Snow Man lit it.

"Painted River told us to sit around the circle. He talked to us for the next two hours, telling us to prepare ourselves to be open to what would happen next. With the firelight dancing over our faces, we let our defenses down and listened.

"Painted River explained that his first experiences as a young man studying to be a shaman had been among the Navajos. Since then he had conducted ceremonies with many tribes in western North America, Mexico, and even down on the Amazon.

"He said he was adapting his knowledge to fit the Western mind. He would show us how to tap our inner magical universe. We would enter a shamanic consciousness where *anything* could happen. But we should not try think of it or explain it. We should just go with it. If we saw strange or surreal events or animals we should not recoil. We were only going to a place where a different kind of reality prevailed.

"He spoke quietly like a man explaining how to do something simple, like paint a room.

" 'I have to ask you to do one thing for me to start,' he said. 'You must consider your former life at an end. You must think for the next several days that you have died.' "

$\triangledown$

Chapter 2

Donald stopped talking. He held his head back and closed his eyes partway to peer out with hooded lids. He set Dillon down beside him and stood up, giving Dillon a pat on the head as the two-year-old went running back into the parlor. Then Donald went to the dining-room closet, where he pulled out his moroccon leather box from behind the cookbooks. He set it in the middle of the table and flipped open the lid.

I could see plastic Baggies of white powder, grass, and mushrooms.

"This is just what I meant," Frederik said, black eyes flashing.

We all looked at him. Anne cut the filming.

"A filmed record to hook us all into something where they can pick us off any time they want. This stuff is nobody's business."

Donald put a hand up to calm Frederik. He winked. "It's not drugs," Donald said. "We can say we got some baking soda here." He lifted up a clear sandwich bag filled with a white powder. "And some oregano here," he held up a freezer size bag filled with an oregano-looking product. "And even A&P's finest mushrooms," he held up the last Baggie so that some kind of mushroom could be clearly seen. "These are just props we made up for Anne's film, who's to know?"

Frederik said nothing but got up from the table and left the room. We heard him climbing the stairs to the second-floor bedrooms. Donald watched him go, then gave a sly smile. "Anything for art," he said.

Anne, trying to keep the proper beat going, started the next scene immediately.

Clark picked up the freezer-size Baggie of grass and took some out, depositing it into cigarette papers. He rolled two joints and then passed one to his left and one to his right. Murph held on to the one that came to him. He put it into his mouth and lit a match, which he held to the end. The paper flared briefly and then the grass glowed with his inhalation. Murph closed his eyes and a few seconds passed as he held drug-laden smoke in his lungs. He passed it to Joan on his right. Joan drew on it and passed it to Donald.

"Yes, Painted River warned us that we had died," Donald said. He held on to his last draw from the reefer for a moment and then exhaled and leaned forward to drink from his wineglass. We drank with him. "He warned us that if we couldn't deal with being with the dead, we should stop that first night."

Donald gestured around with the wineglass. A joint came by me but I passed it on. I agreed with Frederik. But I didn't want to destroy what Anne and Donald had agreed to create. Jennifer still sat at her place watching us. Donald and Joan were adamant that adults should be free to use drugs if they chose. And that the children could be there, just as they would be when the adults drank wine or Scotch.

"Snow Man was the clown in Painted River's court. He danced all around with his weirdly painted face and head of red hair." Donald pushed his hand up over his bald head to pretend he had hair. We all laughed.

"At the end of his talk, Painted River said, 'Watch the stars. Find places there you feel good. Avoid places that are bad.'

"Late in the night, he led us back down the hill. And Snow Man showed us what to do next. We built a sweat lodge, a real Indian sweat lodge, working until dawn by the light of a large fire. On one side was a structure of branches covered with canvas tarps. On the other was a hole in the ground where we had built the fire over some large, loose rocks. During the day we slept and talked more."

He stared straight ahead into the crystal of the wineglass he had set down in front of him, stopping to inhale on one of the joints.

"I can't tell it again," he said finally.

"Sure you can," Elaine said.

"Tell us, go on, Dad," Jennifer said.

There was a chorus of encouragement.

He looked around at all his friends and his little daughter and climbed up to stand over us on his chair. He held his glass up. "That August week was clear and warm," he continued. "There was no moon, and the sky was carpeted with stars." Donald spun slowly, carefully, on his chair, looking at the glass above him. We looked with him as if expecting to see the stars.

Anne cut for a moment and Donald repeated the scene so her B cameraman could take a close-up.

Donald went on. "The vision quest really began. That day we had eaten only a simple Indian stew Painted River cooked for us. In the evening Painted River led us up along the side of the Mohawk hill and Snow Man followed. Painted River told each of us to stop at a place where we felt comfortable. But we had to be out of sight or sound of each other. I was the first to stop. Snow Man gave me a common garden trowel and told me to dig a hole three feet deep to stand in. Then they all disappeared and left me digging. About an hour later, Painted River and Snow Man came back and picked up the trowel. I was to stay in the hole for three nights. No food. No water."

Donald sat down in his chair and pulled his knees up as if he were constrained by a small hole.

Elaine was watching him closely, a slight smile on her face. Josh came running in from the parlor to see what was going on and climbed onto her lap. Jennifer listened as if to a fairy tale. Anne looked very serious, hardly even glancing now at the camera crew.

"I had decided that the Pleiades—the Seven Sisters—was the constellation I would watch for my 'vision.' "

Donald raised his head as if watching the stars.

"All the first night I watched. During the next day I dozed off some and felt hungry a lot. The second night again nothing came at me from the Pleiades. The following day I found I could live with the hunger.

"That third night I felt strangely at peace. The stars were brilliant and the woods around were silent and deep. Really deep. But nothing happened, not in the Pleiades or anywhere else.

"Then, in the morning, Snow Man came around and led us down the hill to the campsite."

"Painted River was there, stirring a kettle of another Indian stew made of roots and natural things he had gathered. We each ate a little to quell the hunger of the three-day fast but not enough to take away the edge that hunger had given us. 'Sleep awhile now,' Painted River then told us, 'and prepare for tonight.' "

Donald stopped as if to catch his breath. "That night Painted River and Snow Man led us back to the top of the hill. Painted River passed out peyote mushrooms to each of us to eat. We formed a circle and Painted River sat in the center and Snow Man on the outside.

" 'Watch the sky,' Painted River said. They were the only words he would say until morning.

"Again the stars were brilliant. Again I felt the well-being I'd come to in my lone vision quest. Sounds came out of the woods around us. I watched the Pleiades attentively. Snow Man began to beat a monotonous rhythm on a drum, a sound we could ride into the 'other reality.' "

Donald bent low over the table, looking around as he spoke. Suddenly he leapt to his feet, and the rest of us jumped in our seats with him in surprise. " 'Hey,' I heard someone shout, 'look at that!' "

Donald looked up and swept his hand across the panorama of the ceiling. "I twisted my head and saw the beginning of my vision. I had been wrong. I should have been

watching Cassiopeia—the Seated Woman—instead of the
Seven Sisters. I saw a woman's face. Mona Lisa's face. And
stars were streaming down the sky on all sides forming her
hair. It went on and on. I blinked and then I saw hundreds,
even thousands of the same face at every point in the sky,
the hair from all of them streaming down to the horizon.

"I heard Painted River chanting to Snow Man's drum-
beat." Donald chanted slowly for a few moments.

I looked around at the others. Clark watched Donald as
if looking for a weakness in the story. Frederik had come
downstairs and was standing in the doorway. Nan stared
down at the tablecloth and looked up nervously. Murph
looked at Donald with amazement on his face. Joan's face
bordered on an expression of severe alarm. Dillon had run
in at the sound of the chanting and stood up on his chair in
rapt attention.

"Suddenly, the women's faces were all gone and I was
soaring." Donald climbed onto his chair again, spread his
arms out like wings, and twisted back and forth, as if he
were a giant bird flying. "I looked out along my wings. They
were black and formed of stars. A black hawk! I flexed and
soared. The group was far below me in a circle on top of the
hill. Painted River was in the middle, the only one looking
up at me."

Suddenly Donald jumped down from the chair and, pushing the china and glassware away in front of him, collapsed
his head and arms across the table. He lay there a moment,
quiet. Then he lifted his head to speak.

"A white sheet had been thrown over my head." He
grabbed a napkin and put it over his head so that only his
mouth was showing. "And I was encased in darkness. Like
that, they led me off the mountain into the woods. We
stopped and I was told to undress. When I removed my shoes
I could feel freshly turned earth under my toes. They had me
lie down on a wooden slab, with the sheet still over me. I
was lowered by ropes into a fresh grave."

Donald sat back limply in his chair. He was quiet for a
moment and the only sound was that of Anne's crew shifting

cameras and lights. Then, just as I was beginning to wonder if he would continue, he sat up, put the napkin on the table and looked around. Clark passed him a fresh reefer and he drew deeply on it. He spoke softly as he let the smoke escape from his lungs.

"You can imagine how frightened I was. Nights under the sky. Soaring, a black hawk. Now darkness and death. The contrast! The horror!

"They began to cover my shrouded body with clumps of fresh earth! One hit me on my forehead, another on the shoulder and another on my chest!"

Donald touched the places where the earth hit him as he told it.

"I was left alone then. It seemed like an eternity until the drum began a slow beat but far away. It came closer and a chant started. As they pined I knew to rise up and climb out."

"I did and I saw the others climbing out of graves too, Joan and Clark and me with our sheets white in the darkness. Figures climbing back into life again."

Donald stopped and settled back into his chair as if finished. He sipped at his wine before he continued.

"Our sheets wrapped around us, we followed Painted River and Snow Man through the woods to the sweat lodge. The fire we built the previous day had been kept burning over the hole we had dug next to the sweat lodge. Now the hole was uncovered and the rocks that filled it were very, very hot. We gathered in a circle around them, and Painted River spoke on our behalf to the four horizons.

"When he had finished Snow Man took a spade and moved the hot rocks from the fire into an identical hole dug in the middle of the sweat lodge. We filed into the lodge and sat around the rocks. Painted River came last with a pail of water. The canvas was closed up so that it was black as the womb inside. Painted River dipped water onto the stones— and he called on our ancestors to hear us. Sweat poured off me. My skin seemed to open up with the heat.

"Then Painted River threw open the canvas, the dawn light flooded in, and we staggered out, renewed, reborn."

Donald paused and looked around the table. Then he
stood up and stretched his hand across toward his daughter.

"Jennifer," he said, "kick your shoes off and get up on the
table."

Holding his hand, Jennifer did as she was told, taking one
step across the dishes on her side to stand in the vacant area
he had created in front of him.

"All that day we ate food Painted River had cooked. And
we danced for hours to a drum Snow Man played. I traveled
down the tunnel, found my hawk, and soared for hours. It
was real.

"At the end, Painted River brought out a magical talisman,
a wing made from the feathers of bald eagles, collected not
from their bodies, but from their nests."

Donald made one arm into a winglike form, holding it up
for all of us to see. "It was nearly six feet long. Each of us
stood in the center of a circle as he slowly swept our aura
with the wing."

Here Donald swept his imaginary wing down over
Jennifer's form.

He looked around the table.

"It gave me and the others the most fantastic sense of
lightness and well-being. I had a sudden surge of strength
and willpower I don't think I ever lost. I felt like Superman."

"You are Superman, right, Dad?" Jennifer said and she
leapt from the table into her father's arms. Everyone at the
table laughed, Donald the hardest of all. Her leap carried us
out of the vision quest and into the present.

"I don't buy it," Murph said. Donald turned toward him,
an amused expression on his face. Joan was turning also and
she looked perplexed. Murph had a frown of disapproval on
his face.

"I don't think you need to go up to mountaintops anymore," Murph said. He looked around the table for support.
"I'd rather be in a nice warm bed. Look, I can rent a video
of a shaman like Painted River and watch him going through
his paces. I can do in a night of watching my VCR what it
took you four days to do. What's the point of it anymore?"

Donald had a look of disappointment on his face.

Murph looked self-satisfied. "Give me a little grass to smoke. A nice warm bed. A woman." He made a small gesture toward Nan. "And I'm set for life. In an evening, I can do it all—anything. Climb the Himalayas, find the source of the Blue Nile, see great white sharks off the Australian barrier reefs. That's my kind of life."

Everyone laughed. Elaine spoke up. "That's it for you, Murph. No freshly dug graves under your bare toes?"

Murph shook his head. He grabbed the joint that was going around. "But grass between my lips," he said, "now that's what I like to feel."

Everyone laughed again.

He inhaled deeply. Then he took the reefer out of his mouth, and exhaled and a cloud of smoke rose from his mouth, obscuring his face.

"That's it, wrap it up," Anne said. The cameras stopped and the crew began to dismantle their equipment.

"Hey," Elaine said, "we were just getting good!"

"I got enough," said Anne, "for a great twenty-minute film. Besides, we were running out of stock in another six minutes and I want to do some retakes of Donald and some archive stuff."

We looked around at one another as if we had just emerged from a dark cave.

Anne and I made the trip from Otis, Massachusetts, to New York City later that night, taking Jennifer and Dillon with us. The others were headed off to ice skate on the pond behind the barn when we left.

$\triangledown$

Chapter 3

THE NEXT NIGHT, a Thursday, was my night to help dish out food to homeless people at our local church. Anne came too, and we brought the kids. Jennifer said the people made her think of birds at the winter bird feeder in the country. Afterward, it was snowing like crazy, so we took our time walking home and throwing snowballs at one another. Then we stopped for hot chocolate.

It was after ten-thirty when we got into our apartment in the brownstone on West Eighty-eighth Street. There was a garbled message from Donald on the answering machine.

"Hello there, Jay. We're just leaving Otis now. Yes, we're driving the old Mustang convertible down through this storm. We're trying to beat the snow, man. I have my reasons. For example, I'm looking right now at a briefcase that's going to knock your socks off. See ya in a couple hours."

It was such a curious message, Anne and I played it a second time, to no further avail. We put Jennifer and Dillon to bed and watched the news to follow the storm.

The next time the phone rang it was late—just after one o'clock. Anne and I had dropped off to sleep, but we were both uneasy and the phone woke me up immediately.

"You decided to go straight home," I said, thinking it could only be Donald and Joan at the other end.

It was Frederik.

"Hello, Jay?" he said, although he knew it was me on the line. His voice seemed to crack as he said my name.

"I haven't heard from Donald and Joan yet," I said, anticipating him. "But they're supposed to be coming in tonight—any time now."

Frederik didn't say anything, and for a minute I thought he had hung up. I could see his black-bearded face and I imagined him closing his dark eyes into narrow slits, which he frequently did as he spoke.

"Yes," I said to break the silence.

"They won't be coming in," Frederik finally said. "Listen to me, Jay. I'm at the country house. The sheriff's office in Falls River, Connecticut, just woke me up. There's been a terrible accident."

Oh, no, I began thinking to myself. Oh no, oh no, oh no. It felt like it was coming out in tiny sounds and rolling along the floor.

"Donald is dead. Joan is dead, too. The Mustang crashed, rolled down into a ravine, exploded into fire. They're gone, Jay. I can't believe I'm telling you this but they are dead."

Frederik started to sob on the phone and I tried to tell him to take it easy, but I found I just sat there listening to his sobbing. My being too quiet woke Anne, and she sat up and looked at me, her face visible in the light from the street. Because of her green eyes she wore lots of green, including a short silk nightshirt that bordered on emerald green. It's the only color I remember in the room. Her long brown hair streamed down her back.

"What's wrong?" she said.

I couldn't speak or cry or anything. I held the receiver out to her. She looked me up and down and took it and held it to her ear. From where I sat Frederik's sobbing carried across the silent room.

"Who is it?" she said into the phone. I could hear what Frederik said because he had to blurt it out loudly between his sobs.

"I can't talk," he said twice, and then he hung up.

* * *

While I dressed, Anne went to get Carol Larsing, my business partner, to watch the kids. Carol hadn't realized when she set me up in the tax business that she would frequently be left with pieces of my personal life too. But I have to confess, she did so magnificently. Carol owns the brownstone we live in. The upper two floors are her apartment; our office and my apartment are on the ground floor. I put up with her weakness, an occasional Havana cigar, and she puts up with all mine.

She didn't have to say anything. She had tears on her cheeks and her pageboy blond hair didn't bounce around her head like it usually does. Anne and I left her there and drove to Connecticut.

I didn't say much on the three-hour trip up to the scene of the accident, halfway between Falls River and Cornwall Bridge on Route 7. I would be okay, but then I'd come back to the idea that Dillon and Jennifer would never be seeing Donald and Joan again. And I would being to lose it. Anne reached over and touched me, holding my hand, until the storm or the road required her to take her hand away to drive. I'd think about the children and then not accept it. How could my brother do this?

A sheriff's car, an ambulance, a fire engine, and a tow truck were lined up in a row along the verge with their lights still flashing in the cold night. Everything was covered with a new crest of snow, and it was still coming down, as well as blowing across the surface of the road. We pulled up along the side of the road opposite them and got out. A sheriff's deputy approached us.

"This is Jay Jasen," Anne said, gesturing toward me.

"Donald Jasen was your brother?" the deputy said. He wasn't happy to see me before they had finished cleaning up. I just nodded. I felt so cold and calm I'm sure he wondered if I felt anything for my brother.

He led us to the edge of the road, and we peered down into the wreckage below us. The Mustang had rolled down a steep incline, going through the guardrail instead of completing the gradual left turn. The spotlight from the fire engine was focused down the hill at the door on the passenger side of the upside-down convertible. I could see the blue flame of a blowtorch at work.

"I'm sorry," the deputy said. "If you want I'll take you to my office."

I shook my head. "They're dead?" I asked not really believing it.

"Yes," he said. He had a wide face and his eyes looked out at me, gauging my reaction. He took hold of my arm and held on firmly.

"I want to know what happened," I said.

"I can see you'd rather know than not. We'll have to cut her out. It looks like the convertible top just collapsed in on them when it rolled. He was lying half out of the car. He's already in the ambulance. Now they're getting the woman. His wife? It's too bad. There's nothing you or I can do."

A shout came from below and two paramedics got out of their warm ambulance and stumbled down the hill through the snow toward the circle of light below.

The deputy continued watching me to see if I was taking it okay. "Looks like he fell asleep at the turn. They went right through the cable guardrail and rolled down the hill. It happened sometime just after eleven-thirty. We know that because we had a patrol unit at the light in Falls River. The guy is a Mustang fanatic and saw the car come through at eleven-thirty. The funny thing is that the Mustang burned later. Somebody reported the fire after midnight . . . just about twelve-fifteen. It shouldn't have burned, a solid car like that. But you get funny things. A gas leak and a hot engine. The gas tank was ruptured in the roll, and they weren't wearing their seat belts. It looks like they died instantly in the roll. They didn't burn up . . . it was before the fire. . . ."

I didn't want to hear any more and I pulled away from him and bounded down the hill toward the wreckage. Tears were freezing on my face but I still felt very calm, very cold. I sensed Anne following me close behind.

When we got to the wreck outlined in the spotlight, I could

see that the Mustang had burned extensively. It lay upside down against two trees that had also burned. Beyond them were some low bushes and then a dark field. The snow blew away from us.

The two paramedics had put something awful into a black plastic body bag and had placed it on the stretcher. I looked away to the field as they carried it back up the hill to the ambulance. When I looked back, the man with the blow-torch was wrapping up his equipment.

"We'll tow this sucker out in the morning," he said to me. "It's not goin' anywhere tonight. We got three more accidents in this storm we gotta hit."

He trudged up the hill away from us. The spotlight went out.

"Come on, Jay," Anne said. She pulled me away from the wreckage. We followed the tow truck driver up the slope. The truck, the fire engine, and the ambulance all left together, and then it was all black down the slope. But Donald and Joan were no longer there anyway.

"If you could get in your car and follow me," the deputy said, "we can get the paperwork out of the way."

Anne and I spent another half hour at the sheriff's office and then checked into a motel. The deputy had done the best he could to help us out of shock. I was surprised because I even laughed twice at easy jokes the deputy attempted. Anne, I remember, looked at me in surprise.

I was exhausted but stared into space as dawn approached, no longer crying, no longer feeling anything except a terrible anger that I couldn't change any of this. It was then that I began to go over Donald's last message.

"I'm looking at a briefcase that's going to knock your socks off."

That idea of a briefcase kept tumbling around in my mind.

Anne was able to sleep, and soon after first light I left her in bed and drove back out to the wreckage of the Mustang. A state trooper was just pulling away in his car. Probably looking forward to some hot coffee after turning the wreck over to the tow truck driver. The tow truck had backed up to the verge, and the driver was down there hooking up some cables. I could see he was a young guy. He wore a red hunting cap with the earflaps down and a green parka soiled with oil. I parked and walked slowly down through the snow.

There was nothing I could do. I left the driver hooking up his cables and wandered off across the field, pulling the collar of my shearling coat up around my ears and hunching over against the wind with my gloved hands deep in my pockets. I came to a frozen stream lined by small hardwoods. Gusty wind carried snow across the surface so that it moved like bubbling water. I walked along, watching the snow flow ahead of me, thinking nothing. Suddenly I began to stomp on the ice, trying to break it. It was solid. I began to pick up stones from an exposed bank and throw them down on the ice. Then I grabbed a heavy dead limb and used it like a sledgehammer. The ice wouldn't break, which made me more and more angry. At last I was smashing into one spot, chipping off little pieces.

When I looked back, I saw the tow truck driver was back on top of the verge by the road. He stood there watching me. Something clicked and I went running back across the field. I ran fast enough to beat the tow truck driver to the wreck. He came down to where I was standing alone in the field. First, I said, I wanted to see if we could get into the Mustang. He said it wasn't possible. The state police required it to be towed to the barracks in Canaan. The trooper had left and I'd have to go to the barracks. He went about hooking up his winch to right the car. After the Mustang was pulled over, I looked into the backseat and found a suitcase. I pulled it out of the wreck and it fell open. Some badly charred clothes dropped to the ground, as did some earrings and a necklace that had belonged to Joan. I stuffed it all back in the case and threw it into the car again. The driver was shouting at me from up the hill to get away. The trunk lid had popped and I looked into it. Inside I saw a badly burned briefcase. Stupidly, I pulled it out and tried to open it. After meeting with some initial resistance, I pried the top open.

Inside was Donald's surprise, or what was left of it. As I

opened the case, a bunch of charred paper blew off across the field. A piece hit me and I looked at it. It was a nearly perfect circle, the edges having all been burned away—a picture of U. S. Grant from the center of a fifty-dollar bill. The tow truck driver came running down at me screaming, but he saw what was happening. He and I lifted our heads and locked eyes at the same time. What the hell? The briefcase was stuffed full of burned money! I bent forward and closed it as well as I could. But several thousand had gone away with that first gust of wind. Not that anyone could ever tell how much had been in the briefcase for starters. The driver went racing crazily across the field trying to gather up the little bits of charcoaled paper. He gave up after a few seconds as the money scattered ahead of him. While he was doing that, I took off my shearling coat and wrapped it around the briefcase for the walk back to my car. I was freezing by the time I slipped into the driver's seat and gently laid the briefcase beside me. There was a solid knock on the window and I looked out to see the red-capped tow truck driver. I rolled the window down a few inches.

"You can't take that away," he said. "The state troopers are going to want to take a look at it."

"Are you a cop?" I asked.

He shook his head. "But the trooper left me in charge."

"Then I'll take responsibility for it," I said, and I pulled away from him. I saw him in the rearview mirror staring after me and I knew I had made some trouble for myself.

Chapter 4

BY THE TIME ANNE had I got home, a Connecticut state trooper had already called.

Carol had taken the call and she met us at the door.

"Sergeant Ross Harris," Carol told us, twisting her head and swinging her blond hair, "and I quote with his tired Scottish accent. 'I dunna know what Mr. Jasen would be thinking of, running off with that wee bit of cash. It's $500,000, and we'll be looking for him to have it back up here by the stroke of twelve tonight.' " Carol looked from me to Anne and back. "What $500,000 is he talking about, Jay?"

Shit, I thought, that much. And how the hell do they know?

I was carrying my coat with the burned briefcase and cash wrapped in it under one arm. I walked past her and through into our office and dumped the goods on top of my desk.

"Where are the kids?" I asked.

Carol gestured toward the other rooms with her head. "Jennifer's watching TV in your bedroom. Dillon's actually taking a nap in the back."

"They know anything yet?"

Carol shook her head. "No. I thought I should wait until you got home."

I turned my attention back to my surprise package and

opened it up very, very carefully. My coat was going to need a good cleaning.

Carol sniffed the air. "What'd you bring home, Jay? A package of burned trash?" Both she and Anne moved closer so that they were hovering over my desk.

Anne knew what to except, but Carol gave a startled gasp when she realized she was looking at a full briefcase of burned cash. It smelled like trash, but it was still worth many, many thousands. But $500,000?

"What's going on, Jay?" Carol said. "Where did all this money come from?"

"The trunk of Donald and Joan's car."

Just then we heard the patter of Dillon's little feet. His dimpled face topped with dark red hair peered around the doorjamb at us. I felt my heart drop.

"Everything else has to wait," I said, folding my coat back over the cash and briefcase. "I think we have to tell Dillon and Jennifer now."

Anne swung her head from side to side, not in disagreement, but in disbelief as to the magnitude of what had happened. Anne went into our bedroom, calling to Jennifer. As Donald's brother and their uncle, I would be the one to break the news.

Telling the children was horrible. There wasn't any way that two-year-old Dillon was going to understand. But Jennifer was six. Anne held Dillon on her lap and Jennifer sat beside me on the couch where I could hug her. Carol sat on the floor facing us.

"What's wrong, Jay?" Jennifer asked. She had brown curly hair and blue eyes like Joan's. She liked to put "rainbow sprinkle" barrettes in her hair.

Dillon had no idea what was going to happen and was showing his cute dimples, basking in the sudden attention.

"I have to tell you some very sad news," I said. I stumbled around for a minute. How could I say it best? What was the correct way to tell a child both her parents were dead?

"Your parents were supposed to come home late last night. But they had an accident on the way, Jennifer. It was a bad accident. Your mother and father can't come home."

I had to stop. I didn't know what to say next so I didn't
say anything. Jennifer looked up at me.

"Did they die, Jay?" she asked.

Surprised, I could only nod. I couldn't even get out a yes.

I don't know what Jennifer's concept of death was. I knew
she had a pet cat killed by a car at the country house. I knew
she had never dealt with human death before. She sat as if
holding her breath for a few moments. I held mine too, waiting for her to say something as I hugged her small body close
to me. Carol and Anne seemed to be suspended in that same
frozen time. Anne held Dillon tightly to her. Carol's knuckles turned white where she gripped the front of her knees.
Our eyes met over the children, and we waited for Jennifer
to react. And then Jennifer began to cry and so did I and then
Anne and then Carol. Little Dillon may not have understood
what had happened, but he felt our emotion and cried with
us. We all sat there crying together, not hysterically, just
together and I knew Jennifer was going to be all right. And
I knew I was going to be all right too.

Jennifer had lots of questions about death. They were the
kinds of questions I had given up asking myself, and I couldn't
answer them for her. Where did they go? What was there?
Were they going to be happy? And last, were she and Dillon
going to have to eat at the church with the homeless people?

"Jennifer," I told her, "I'm going to be your new father.
Dillon's too."

Jennifer pulled away from me. Then she smiled with her
blue eyes still moist. "You can't be my father, Jay," she said.

"I can't?" I said, a little shocked.

"Don't be silly. You're my uncle, not my dad."

It was the kind of logic that made me smile and made me
think I'd have to be careful what I said.

"You're right, Jennifer," I said, "I am your uncle and a
damn good one too."

After that, Anne and I cooked the kids their favorite dinner—spaghetti and meatballs—and we sat around the table
remembering various things we liked about Donald and
Joan.

After dinner, it was obvious that the children were exhausted and so were we. Anne and I sat with them the very short while it took them both to fall asleep.

Carol was busy in the front office and looked at us as we came in, then sat in the brown leather recliner.

"Well, Jay, it's beginning to look worse and worse. I mean, I don't want to say this because I know how we all hate the 'pigs.' But don't you think there is a chance Donald and Joan were involved in something illegal? Drugs maybe?"

"Drugs!" Anne said.

The three of us looked at the cash on my desk.

"I didn't want to think about it," I said.

Carol and Anne looked as helpless as I felt.

"You know I'd be the last person to say this if I didn't think it was necessary," she said, "but I think you ought to give Bruce Scarf a call."

Bruce Scarf. It took my breath away to think I would have to call on Bruce in his professional capacity. Bruce Scarf worked as a homicide detective in an East Side precinct of the NYPD.

"But we aren't talking about murder here," I said. "We're talking about finding a briefcase full of cash in the trunk of their car and some cops in Connecticut saying it was $500,000. If I thought my brother and his wife were murdered, I'd want to talk to Bruce Scarf."

Anne took Carol's side. "Jay, you took evidence from the scene of a police investigation. You don't know what kind of trouble you might be in. Since you don't have a criminal lawyer, I think Carol's right. It can't hurt to call Bruce."

I squirmed a little bit and then I said, "Okay, let's call him."

One very admirable quality about Carol is that she does not procrastinate. She got up and walked right to the phone on her desk. Moments later she had Bruce on the phone. He was at home on a Friday evening.

Bruce is very big and very black. He looks a little bit like the heavyweight boxer George Foreman. He even won a few fights in Golden Gloves competition as a kid. I met him

watching the sixth game of the 1986 World Series. It was a
Saturday night and Bruce and I were both losing a lot of
money going in to the tenth inning until Bill Buckner blew
Boston's win over the Mets by letting the ball roll between
his legs. We were at the West End Café—the old West End—
and we each let some money roll across the bar after the win.
We've been friends ever since.

"Bruce," I said, "I've got some trouble here. I mean some
real trouble. I need your help."

"How much you need, buddy?" He had one of those deep
bass voices that roll around a room and come right back at
you even over a telephone line.

I had to smile. "Sorry, it's worse than that. My brother
and his wife died in a car accident last night. I took a briefcase full of money from the wreck and now the cops in Connecticut are—"

"Whoa, slow down," Bruce said. I heard him pause and
take a very deep breath himself. "You have to take things as
they come. Your brother and sister-in-law *both* died?"

"Yes," I said.

"Wow, man, I am really sorry. He was a great dude. She
was a great lady. I'm sorry for you. What happened with the
kids?"

I guess in Bruce's job he has to make a point of looking
at the human side of death or he'd soon be overwhelmed by
the never-ending corpses with anonymously tagged toes. I
appreciated his concern. We talked family for a few minutes.
Then he got down to business.

"What makes you believe you've got yourself into a jam?"

I started to tell him about the cash again. But he stopped
me in the middle.

"Listen, bro," he said, "I'm out of here in twenty minutes
and I'm going to be pounding on your front door ten minutes
after that. You just hold on to everything until the man
arrives."

He left me clutching the phone feeling very glad he was
my friend.

$\triangledown$

Chapter 5

Bruce took more than an hour to make it to the office after I spoke to him. Anne had turned in, exhausted from the events of the day and from driving to and from the accident. Bruce took up even more space than Clark. I suppose he really looked more like bass player Charley Mingus than like George Foreman. He had on darkly tinted glasses that made him appear more formidable than he actually was. He said it helped his image as a homicide detective—especially in interrogations—to have his large and potentially threatening form peering down at a suspect from behind almost dark glasses.

"Hey, my man," he said as I opened the door to him. He grabbed my hand and gave it the double shake he always used. "What's happening? Why didn't you call me about your brother and his wife earlier? Sounds to me like you had a rough time of it over there." He shook his head and took off his glasses to wipe his brow, then put them back on. "It's unbelievable."

I let him give me his coat, a long, black leather one in an extra-extra-large double-breasted size that had epaulets on the shoulders and a wide belt at the waist. He had a gold pendant that said "Debbie" on a gold chain around his neck. He wore plain black wool slacks and a white linen

31

dress shirt open three buttons at the collar and rolled back at the French cuffs.

"Okay," he said, "get me cold ale and I'll listen to your sad tale. All night if I gotta."

I walked him into my office. The French doors between Carol's office and mine were open and Carol was sitting at my desk.

"Hi, Brucie," she said, waving to him but not getting up. "How's everything in Fascist central?"

Bruce smiled back at her as he let himself down into the brown leather recliner. "We're just hanging in there waiting for you to step out of line."

He sat with his flat feet on the floor and used his thumb and forefinger on each hand to pull up on his slacks so that the crease was straight to each knee. He had a gold Rolex on his left wrist and a couple of gold rings on his fingers. He wore black cowboy boots that had a fleur-de-lis design and were shined to such a high gloss you could see your face.

"You want to get the beers," I asked Carol, "or would you prefer I did?"

"No problem," Carol said smiling sweetly at Bruce. "I wouldn't want to risk being left alone with a pole-leeceman."

Bruce laughed as Carol left the room. The kidding around had always been the gem of their relationship although it sometimes seemed on the verge of getting out of hand.

Carol came back carrying three bottles of Amstel Light. She gave one to each of us and sat down, this time at her own desk. Bruce looked it over. "Light?" he said.

"You be good and drink that, maybe we'll have some real stuff for you," Carol told him.

Bruce took a chug that drained half the bottle.

"Okay," he said, "I'm ready."

I settled back into the swivel chair at my desk and began at the beginning. I told about how we had been in the country for Anne to film the dinner party two nights before and brought the children home with us that night. Donald and Joan had planned to come home to their apartment in the city two days later. But, in a message left on my answering machine, Donald said that they were driving back in the storm. Also, that he was looking at a briefcase that "would knock my socks off."

I mentioned Frederik's call just after one o'clock. Then how Anne and I drove up to the scene and how the next morning I'd slipped the briefcase out of the trunk and brought it home. Now Sergeant Ross Harris and the Connecticut State Police wanted $500,000.

Bruce had finished the beer and hadn't even thought to ask for more.

"You mean you got a half-million dollars here?" Bruce said when I was done.

I pointed to my coat on top of my desk. "What I've got is burned up. I don't know where the half-million number comes from."

He stood up then and came over still carrying the empty Amstel in one hand. Once more I unwrapped my package.

Bruce gave a whistle when he saw the cash. "Hey, my man," he said, "you *really* got something there."

"What do you think, Bruce?"

Bruce turned away from where we stood at the desk and said nothing, walking over to the window and looking out onto West Eighty-eighth Street as if he expected to find some answers there.

Carol and I waited, not wanting to interrupt his train of thought.

"Yeah," he said finally, turning back to us. "Yeah, I'd say you've got yourself a pack of trouble here. I'd say your brother and his wife were into something."

"What should we do?" I asked him.

Bruce looked from me to Carol and then held up the beer bottle. "Get me something that's real—not this light shit."

Carol took the bottle from him and disappeared. He walked back to the recliner and sat down again, this time pushing it back until he felt comfortable.

"We gotta take some action," he said.

I nodded. Carol came back with a Becks for Bruce.

"Ah, that's my girl," Bruce said. He smacked his lips and

took a long chug. "If you sit down you'll just have to get up and get me another one," he said.

Carol smiled sweetly at him and let herself fall gently onto the office couch.

"What should be done, Bruce?" I asked.

"What's going to happen is that some judge in Connecticut is going to issue a search warrant based on their witness that you took this money from the scene. Then they send the warrant down here to get some judge to allow action on it locally. At that point some of my buddies show up here around tomorrow afternoon to search and seize. Maybe they haul you away too. It depends on how much you got their backs up."

Bruce took his second chug from the beer. He held up the bottle and peered into it, shaking it slightly. I grabbed it from him and went for another one. When I got back, Bruce and Carol were laughing together. It was a good sign.

"What to do with you and this alleged $500,000 you took from the trunk of your brother's car is a problem," Bruce said after he'd accepted a fresh beer. "Why didn't you just leave it with the cops at the scene of the accident?"

Carol answered for me. "Come on, Brucie, get real. Would you?"

Bruce smiled widely then, a black face with dark glasses showing a Cheshire cat row of white teeth. "I see. But now you gotta pay the man.

"Wait," I said, "it's a fair question. But I don't think I can give you a smart answer. I was angry at the time. Mad that Donald and Joan were dead. Mad that my own life seemed to be irretrievably messed up. I saw that money and I knew that if I left it with the cops it could be years before the kids would see it again. I grabbed it while it was grabbable and now I'm stuck with the consequences."

Bruce let out a sigh. "Okay," he said. "That's what it is. Let me call up there in the morning. I'll see what's going on." He gestured to the money. "I don't want to touch that shit myself. Too many complications. Let me tell you what a guy I know did in a similar situation. He sent the damaged cash off to the U.S. Treasury for salvage assessment. That way it

wasn't here—there—when the search and rescue team
showed up. He took plenty of photographs in case he needed
them for a court case first."

Bruce took a second swallow from the beer that seemed
to drain the bottle. " 'Course I couldn't recommend such an
action." Then he got to his feet.

"I gotta get back to Debbie," he said.

"We know her?" Carol said.

Bruce gave another Cheshire cat smile. "I hope not," he
said. "You might know her old man too."

There was nothing we could do but laugh after a comment
like that, but it sounded to me like Bruce was getting himself
into another emotional jam. I walked him to the hallway
and helped him with his coat. He turned to me as he opened
the door.

"We gotta have a few drinks soon and go over stuff," he
said.

"I know, I know," I said. "I got this damn tax business
holding me down for the next couple of months, then I'm
ready."

"I'll be calling you tomorrow," Bruce went on, "with the
results of my rapping with Connecticut."

He turned back one last time. "Take care," Bruce said,
giving me a wave, and he was gone. But I had a sense that
he really meant the "take care" part.

Back in the office, Carol was already snapping some flash
photos of our pile of trash money.

"It's been one hell of a day," she said, stopping for a moment. "You know I usually worry half of every night, but
tonight I think I'll just sleep."

"I know what you mean," I said. "Nothing like emotion
to take everything out of you."

Still carrying the camera, Carol went to the door, turning
just before she went out into the hallway. "If tax season is
going to be this tough, I think I'll quit now. It's too much."

"I think we just have to roll with the breakers for a few
days," I said, "then maybe the weather will clear. It can't
stay like this."

She just nodded and closed the door behind her. I heard her footsteps on the stairs and then I turned to my own bed.

Anne woke up as I came into the bedroom.

"Everything okay, Jay?" she mumbled half asleep.

"Well, we got Bruce Scarf on our side," I told her. "That feels like it goes a long way to being okay."

I took off my clothes and crawled in beside her, nearly asleep before my head hit the pillow when there was a tiny knock on our door.

"Just a second," I said, and I jumped up and put on the bottoms to some old gray cotton pajamas I had. I opened the door while Anne watched from the bed.

Jennifer stood there with Dillon in front of her. She had her arms around him, hugging him to her as they looked in at us. Dillon had a faint smile that showed his dimples and looked cute as a puppy with his dark red hair and wide brown eyes.

"Could we please sleep in here with you guys tonight?" Jennifer asked.

I looked back at Anne.

"Sure," Anne said. "I think we'd all feel better."

"Hop in," I said. And in a few moments the lights were out and the two kids were fast asleep snuggled right between two of us.

Anne woke up in the middle of the night and shook me hard.

"What is it?" I asked, awake but still asleep too, my brother's image in my mind trying to speak to me.

"I feel so bad," Anne whispered. The forms of the two children fast asleep were between us.

"I know," I said.

She was sitting up looking at the darkness directly in front of her, her arms wrapped around her knees, her long hair streaming down her back.

"No. I mean about the film. You remember what the central story told in the film was? I had Donald describe the night they died and they did die. I feel so guilty."

I turned on the beside reading light and looked at her. Her green eyes were wet with tears that also ran down her cheeks.

"I feel responsible," she said. "Somehow I was responsible for them dying."

It was my turn to comfort her. I walked around the bed to avoid waking the children and sat beside her, hugging her tight. Her tears made a wet spot on my shoulder.

"I look at it differently," I told her. "The film was made at the right time. Donald talks about the night he died. But remember it wasn't the night he died. It was the night he feels they were reborn with a new consciousness. It was a night that shaped the rest of their lives."

Anne had stopped crying and a little smile even crossed her lips. "You really think so?"

"Yes," I said. "You should be proud of yourself, not guilty."

I could feel the tension draining from her muscles as I held her. We lay down again together on her side of the bed and, holding on to each other loosely, went to sleep.

The next morning, the males were up early while the females slept. Dillon and I had cereal and juice and I also had coffee. Then I dressed him in his mittens, boots, and snowsuit, grabbed an old coat—the shearling was still wrapped around the briefcase—and the two of us went for a walk in Riverside Park. Because he was still too young to understand, Dillon made the perfect Freudian psychoanalyst. He never responded to anything I said.

About an inch of snow had fallen overnight. Just enough to cover the dirt and slush left from the deadly storm of the night before that. Dillon had the concept but not the skill for making and throwing snowballs. He remembered us throwing snowballs on the way home from the church two nights before. It was reassuring to have a two-year-old trying to pepper me with featherweight snowballs. He was laughing. Me too. Finally I sat down on a park bench where I could see the Hudson River. He circled around me, playing in the snow. We were alone except for an occasional jogger.

"Well, Dillon," I said, "life has taken a strange turn. Suddenly it looks like I'm a father instead of an uncle."

Dillon let me have it with another snowball, which hit me like a shower of snowflakes.

"I think I'm in love with Anne. But I don't think she's ready for this instant motherhood." I paused for a moment, considering. "I don't think she's even ready to be a wife—not yet, anyway."

Somewhere Dillon had gotten hold of a piece of ice and he chucked it at me. Luckily, it went flying up and over my left shoulder. The kid had a good arm.

I showered him with some loose snow in retaliation and he laughed and reached for more.

On the Hudson River a tugboat pushed a barge upstream.

"Look, Tuffy Tugboat," I said through another shower of snowball flakes. I hoisted Dillon up and pointed at the boat.

"Tuffy Tugboat," I said again.

"He's going to the Little Red Lighthouse?" Dillon asked, pointing to the boat. "Tuffy Tugboat going home now."

I set him down and sighed deeply. I wished Dillon could go home too. He climbed up on the bench beside me and sat in my lap.

"And where the hell did your parents get $500,000?" I asked, playing a tug of war with him. Finally I let him pull me off the bench, and both of us tumbled into a soft pile on the snow. Dillon laughed uproariously, his dimples and wide brown eyes turning him elfin right before my eyes.

I sat up suddenly and repeated again. "Where the hell did . . . You know, Dillon, that would be one hell of a tax bill!"

He looked up at me. "Ax bill," he said dutifully.

"Yeah, taxes on $500,000 income would be about $200,000, including New York State and City."

He looked at me with a quizzical expression but it didn't stop me.

"But what if there's only $100,000 left in identifiable cash?" I went on, touching the tip of his nose to make my point. "Then your parents could take a $400,000 casualty loss and only pay $60,000 in taxes. That would leave you and Jennifer with $40,000."

My mind was racing ahead to a new point. Wait a second, I thought, the trooper said they died in the crash at about eleven-thirty but the fire didn't start until after midnight. That meant the $500,000—if it was income—was fully taxable to Donald and Joan on their final income tax return. But the loss by fire wouldn't be deductible. The loss occurred in the day after they died—after midnight. So the loss was to their estate. It wouldn't apply to their taxes before death. The kids could owe up to $200,000 in taxes and might have less than $100,000 of the burned money left to pay it. Even the children's share of the Otis house might have to be sold to pay the taxes!

Dillon ran and jumped right at me and I caught him in midair.

"Dillon, old man," I said, "it's just possible that this $500,000 is going to cost you and Jennifer everything."

I gave him the biggest hug I could so that he wouldn't see how grim that thought made me feel.

Then there was the drug angle. If the IRS assumed this was drug income they might come in and seize everything for the taxes and also confiscate the salvaged money as "tainted" cash. That's how drug dealers were usually nabbed, starting with Al Capone—not for drug dealing but for taxes.

Dillon got up and ran way from where I sat on the ground, collected some more snow, and came back to shower me with it.

"So tell me, Dillon, is the $500,000 income? People only pay taxes on income."

I got to my feet and brushed off the snow. Dillon laughed at me. "You look funny, Uncle Jay."

"So," I said, "you didn't tell me yet. Where did they get the money?"

Dillon opened his mittens to show empty hands. "All gone," he said.

"Come on," I said to him, "I'll race you home."

Dillon won.

$\triangledown$

Chapter 6

'HI," CLARK SAID from where he filled the kitchen door, watching as Dillon and I came in. He waved a mug of coffee at me while in midbite of a red-jelly-covered piece of toast. As always, he wore his bib overalls, a red checkered flannel shirt and brown cowboy boots scuffed beyond belief with a fleur-de-lis stitch design like Scarf's. His long brown ponytail swung behind his head.

Jennifer and Anne sat at the small breakfast nook in the kitchen, eating and talking. Clark's 260 pound, six-foot-two frame wouldn't fit at the nook.

"You heard?" I said to Clark.

He nodded. "I got back to the Otis house just after Frederik called you. I'd gone over to my mother's house in Connecticut that morning. I must have been driving back to Otis up Route 8 just as they were getting in trouble over on Route 7. Anne just told me some of what happened at Falls River."

He paused, and I could see him trying to catch up with his feelings. His brown eyes looked away from me and back. He put down the toast and coffee and we hugged each other tightly. Then he scooped up Dillon, who laughed with delight, giving Clark the full two-dimple treatment.

Clark owned the Otis house along with Frederik, Donald, and Joan. But for him it was also home year-round. He still lived the idea of a commune—by himself. He planted orchards and truck gardens that sustained everyone for the summer and part of the autumn and even into the winter.

After he had set Dillon down, he leaned against the sink and looked at me again. He filled the kitchen. I poured myself a mug of coffee and topped his up again.

Clark never said much. He was wordless now, apparently just wanting to be with us.

"It's the end of twenty years together," he said at last. "I don't know what I'm going to do."

"Everything's going to be okay," I said. I didn't believe it though.

Clark set down his coffee and began to pace around the kitchen in a small circle. There was barely room for the rest of us to be in there with him. Dillon began to follow in his footsteps, a midget following a giant. It was hilarious. Clark said nothing, just trundled back and forth with Dillon's smiling dimples behind him. Big bear; little bear. Pooh and Piglet. Jennifer was the one who started to laugh first and in a minute we were all laughing, even Clark. We laughed ourselves silly. It was the same reflex as the crying but we laughed and laughed. Finally I wiped the tears from my eyes, and, although I couldn't speak without breaking into laughter again, I managed to drag Clark out of the kitchen and into the front office. He collapsed hysterically into the brown recliner. We tried unsuccessfully to speak a couple of times before we could control it.

"Do you know about the money?" I was finally able to ask him. Clark shook his head.

This time I did not open up my coat. "Donald and Joan were carrying $500,000 in cash in the trunk of the Mustang."

I think it was a good minute before Clark spoke.

"Drugs?"

I shrugged to show it could be anything as far as I was concerned.

"He scored some good coke before Christmas," Clark said. He smiled, remembering.

I was the odd man out on drugs. Everybody else in the

group was "drug oriented," as Donald used to say. Even
Anne joined in sometimes. I didn't like it but if I asked
anybody about it, a defensive wall was set up. "There are no
addicts," Donald claimed. I had my doubts about Clark.
Sometimes I also had my doubts about Frederik. Elaine too.
But I'd learned to keep them to myself. One of Joan's best
friends had a husband who worked in a federal prosecutor's
office. Donald refused ever to let Joan's friend or her husband
into his home. In Donald's view, the man was a representa-
tive of Fascist repression. Drugs equaled individual freedom.
Donald favored medical intervention on drugs rather than
legal intervention. But even there, he felt the individual had
a right to destroy his own body.

I disagreed with him violently. But we put our differences
aside in the interests of family. We didn't discuss it and none
of them did much drugs when I was around.

Except on the night of Anne's filming, when Donald had
brought out his moroccon box. He knew it was part of the
culture she was trying to capture in that film and so I could
hardly complain.

"That was nice coke," Clark repeated. He was still smiling.

"So what," I said. Clark sometimes annoyed me. He could
sit back and examine his navel all day.

Clark shrugged. "Maybe he got cut in as a runner. Maybe
he brought a lot of dope up from the city. Maybe he was just
carrying the cash back. We all know he wasn't a dealer. But
a lot of people knew him. You think they wouldn't trust him
to carry up the goods and bring back the cash? Anybody
would trust Donald. Especially if you'd been selling to him
for five years. Call his contact."

Unfortunately, Clark's idea was not as cockamamy as I
would have liked to believe. I had never wanted to know who
Donald got the drugs from. Now I'd have to find out.

"On second thought, I think I'd let his dealer call you,"
Clark volunteered before I could say anything.

I looked at him puzzled.

His ponytail was curved down over one shoulder onto his
red checkered shirt and he put a hand up and stroked it once.

"If they're missing money, they might never claim it. No one needs to know it wasn't burned up in the accident. Even if they found out, it's just too complicated to step forward. What do they say, 'Hey, give me back my drug money?' No. I think they write it off."

Clark knew a thing or two about this sort of thing, and I saw immediately that I'd follow his advice for the time being. Although, because of the tax situation, I would rather it were someone else's money and not Donald and Joan's. And I didn't want anything to do with drug money. For a second I wanted to shout at Clark. I wanted to say, Why the hell couldn't you guys get away from that stuff. I don't want my life ruined with tainted money.

But the phone rang and Carol came breezing into the office just at that point. She picked up the phone.

"It's Frank Murphy," she said, passing it to me.

Good old Murph. He and Nan had been stringers to the Otis commune ever since the group had bought the house there. Murph's work as the postmaster for the one-room post office made him a natural recipient of local gossip. He came to dinner a lot, smoked Donald's dope, and generally sat wide-eyed watching the comings and goings of the artists, writers, and filmmakers who passed through.

I could imagine him hunched over his phone, a worried look on his face, eyes behind horn-rimmed glasses, running one hand nervously through his thinning brown hair as he talked. A thick brown mustache that always needed a trim covered his upper lip.

"Did you hear?" I asked him.

"Yes," he said. "Frederik told us before he left yesterday. Nan and I are terribly upset. We want to know if there is anything we can do."

"It was horrible," I told him. "But we think they were killed instantly when the car rolled."

"What can we do?" Murph asked again.

Their house faced the Otis house. It was a two-story white frame structure across the road from the bottom of the commune's long driveway.

Murph went on. "It's impossible to believe that just twenty-four hours before they died we were all sitting around the table, eating, drinking, talking about everything. Oh, christ, Jay, why do things like this happen?"

I let the silence grow on the phone for a moment.

"Did you hear about the money?" I asked him.

There was a pause. "Money?" Murph said.

"Yes. The police claim Donald and Joan had $500,000 in a briefcase in the trunk."

If no one else knew, I could hardly expect Murph to know. He and Nan were fellow travelers, not members of the group. Nobody ever told them the whole story about anything, and they didn't want to know. Murph was inclined to reach for another Scotch or another joint at those Otis dinners rather than respond to the intellectual opinions that flew around the table.

Nan watched and worried about how many Scotches or joints Murph was having. She was a plain round-faced woman partial to drab print housedresses. She wore no jewelry except for her wedding band.

"Donald had $500,000 in the trunk?" Murph asked in awe. "Where did it come from?"

"We don't know," I told him. "I thought there was a chance you or Nan might.

"Just a second," Murph said and he muffled the phone with his hand. In a moment he came back on and he laughed for the first time in our conversation.

"My God, Jay, the kids are rich."

Sure, I thought to myself, unless it works out that they owe a couple hundred grand to the IRS and have nothing to pay with. But to Murph I just said it was more complicated than that. A lot of the money had burned up in the crash and we had to get the U.S. Treasury to tell us the value of the money that was left.

"And," I added, "it's important we find out where the money came from."

"Came from?" Murph said. "What's it matter where it came from?"

"It's complicated," I repeated. "I'll tell you all about it later. The IRS may get all that's left and more. There's not enough to pay the taxes. And then, of course, the police are going to want to know where it came from."

"Oh," Murph said. There was quiet for a moment. "What about the film? We want to see it."

"That's Anne's department. I think she wants to show everybody the rough cuts as soon as possible. But she doesn't even get the film back until next week. We haven't even talked about it since the accident."

I told Murph that we'd be in touch.

While I was talking, Carol had gone out and come back with a cardboard packing box. She opened up my coat and gently transferred the briefcase into the box. Clark stood up and I could see the amazed expression on his face as he got a glimpse of the cash. Carol bundled it all up, leaving the top open for the moment.

As I hung up, she was addressing it to the Bureau of Engraving and Printing at the U.S. Treasury in Washington, D.C.

"What's that?" I asked.

"It's for the mutilated money people at the Treasury."

Carol was great as a business partner because she always handled things on an *A, B, C* basis.

"We've got to get this stuff out of here before the search and seize folks show up. Remember what Bruce said his *friend* did?"

I nodded.

"And how it's better to hide it than for the U.S. government to have possession." She swung around and went back to her desk where she flicked on her computer and typed a short letter. Then she printed it and brought it back to me.

"Here's the letter you have to send with it. Just sign."

I looked at the letter. It said I was enclosing burned currency, which I believed had an original value of $500,000. I requested their estimate of the salvage value. It said the check should be made out to the estate of Donald Jasen."

"It's free and they don't even get into ownership."

I signed the letter. She slipped it in with the money and began to seal the box carefully with packing tape. When she'd finished she handed it to me.

"Okay," she said, "off you go. They only accept registered mail, so you have to take it to the post office. And we've got to get it out of here quick."

She smiled a pixielike smile at me, twinkling her blue eyes and letting her blond hair swing around her shoulders.

"Come on, Clark," I said. "You can see to it I make it to the post office safely."

Just as I was about to go out the door, Anne shouted for me to stop, and Jennifer came running down the hall. She handed me a list on a piece of notepaper.

"You have to go to our house," Jennifer said, "and pick up this stuff for Dillon and me."

I looked at the list. There was a Ninja Turtle doll, two teddy bears, one Barbie, a fire engine, and then a list of clothes.

"Jennifer, you guys want this stuff, you got it." I gave her a hug and waved to Anne. Clark gave them both hugs and then called for Dillon who came running out. Clark swept him up into the air and kissed him.

Clark gave me a ride in his Dodge pickup to the post office, where he dropped me before heading back to Otis. After the usual half hour in line, I safely registered the package and it was on its way to the U.S. Treasury.

Then I went over to Donald and Joan's apartment on West Ninety-fourth Street, near Amsterdam. I intended just to check their mail and pick up the toys and clothes for the children. I always carried keys to their apartment on a ring with my own, but I didn't need them once I'd gotten into the building—the door to the apartment was open.

They had been robbed.

The place felt as though there'd been a hurried search for valuables by burglars. Dresser drawers were scattered and clothes were tossed onto the floor. At first I had the horrible sense that someone was still there behind the door to each room waiting to hit me over the head or worse. But that feeling passed and was replaced with a new one—anger. Was this one of those grave robber deals—a thief who watches the news for out-of-town deaths and heads for an apartment before the family does? Didn't we have enough trouble without this?

How could I figure out what had been taken? Donald or Joan would have known what was missing. In this case, making a list of what had been stolen would take a lot of guesswork.

I called Bruce Scarf. Luckily, he was in his office.

"This mean the search and seize boys are there?" he said when he got on the line.

"It's worse than that," I said. "I'm at Donald and Joan's apartment. But I was beaten here. They've been robbed."

Bruce let out a low whistle. "You just don't know how to stop trouble once it starts, do you," he said.

"I'm over my head, Bruce," I told him.

"Hold on a second," he said. I waited, looking around me at the mess. I moved toward the desk and nearly jumped out of my skin when someone moved toward me on the other side of the room. But it was my own reflection in a full-length closet mirror. I looked a fright—my brown hair messed up as if I'd just awakened and my brown eyes appearing deep and haggard. I hadn't shaved that morning or the morning before, so I had a nice shadow. I could see why I scared myself.

"Okay, my man," Bruce said when he came back. "I'd like to get over there. Unhappily we got three homicides last night. So you have to call the precinct. Ask for Detective Garner. He does the B&E's over there. He's good. Tell him you know me. Call me back this afternoon after three o'clock."

I thanked him and got hold of Detective Garner on the first try. Bruce's name worked a kind of magic, and Garner said he was on his way over. Next I called a locksmith to fix the broken lock. Finally, while I waited, I called Carol.

"Wow" was all she could say when she heard the news, "that's incredible. What bad luck." She was quiet for a moment. "Do you think they were looking for $500,000?"

It was my turn to be quiet. "That's a thought," I said. "It would make things sticky, wouldn't it."

I heard the other line ringing in the background, and Carol said she'd see me later.

Waiting for the police, I busied myself packing up some of the children's things. The thief or thieves hadn't touched the children's room at all. But the rest of the apartment was a wreck. Every drawer had been pulled out and the contents left helter-skelter. The worst was an antique desk in the living room. Not only were their financial records scattered from the drawers, but also hundreds of photographs of them and me and the people and events that had meant something to them over the years.

Detective Garner showed up in about twenty minutes. He looked like a fireplug with a Buster Brown haircut, a fedora, and black gloves. I let him in and he went from room to room surveying the damage. I explained that Donald and Joan had died in a car accident two nights ago. He shook his head in sympathy.

"You have any idea what's missing?" Garner asked, looking at me as if I was somehow suspect in spite of my mention of Bruce's name.

I just shrugged. "It's not my home," I said. "I'll have to go over everything and see what I can remember."

He nodded as if that was a good idea. He wrote down everything I could tell him about the robbery. Then he asked me to come over to the precinct and make a report of the missing goods. He waved and was nearly out the door when he turned back to me.

"It's a strange set of circumstances," he said as if putting it together in his mind for the first time. "Maybe it's just some smart guy who puts together death reports in the paper and apartments without anybody in them."

I nodded as though I thought he was clever to think of it and he was gone. Just then the locksmith arrived, and while he worked I cleaned up the place as best I could. He was long gone before I finished.

The hardest part emotionally was picking up all those

family snapshots. Donald or Joan had organized them so
that there was an album for each year. Each photo had a date
on the back. I stuck them into the album for the correct year.
Then I stacked albums in chronological order. There was an
album for every year except for 1975. It was missing entirely.
I thought at the time that they must have taken it up to the
country house.

There was more trouble at home than I had bargained for.
Carol had a grim look and told me to look in my office. I
found my friend Jerry Barnes sitting in the brown recliner.
Jerry is a special agent at the Internal Revenue Service. He's
nearly bald, wears Coke-bottle-bottom glasses, and has a gut
that won't stop that he's earned from years of drinking beer.

"He won't tell me why he's here," Carol said in annoyance.

"Hi, Jerry," I said. He struggled to his feet and shook my
hand. "What's up?"

"A termination assessment."

Carol and I looked at each other. "A termination assessment," we said together. That was when the IRS came in and
seized everything to prevent a flight of capital to evade taxes.

"What?" I said and then, "Why?"

"It's against the estate of your brother. According to the
IRS people up in Hartford, you may have concealed money
with the intent to evade taxes. There's also a question of
tainted money."

"You mean you're here to seize everything left in my
brother's estate? Left to a two-year-old and a six-year-old?
The house, the cash, the clothes, his fucking guitar?"

"No," Jerry said, waving me off with a raised hand. "I'm
here because I stopped it. I saw it coming through and I
stopped it. I'm here because I'm still your buddy. But I don't
know how long that's going to last if you go around taking
money that might be owed the government in taxes and
might be illicit gain."

Relieved, I sat down at my desk. But he came up beside me.

"I got to take something back," Jerry said.

"The guitar?" I suggested grimly.

He smiled at me. "I know it's been tough on you, Jay," he said. "And I'm sorry about your family. Just tell me when we can expect an accounting and what's the deal on that."

Jerry left feeling moderately happy when we told him that the U.S. Treasury had the burned cash for salvage assessment. He thought he could give us time to file a tax return up through the August extension date if we needed it. I had to be happy with that.

When he'd gone we figured it was time to check in with Bruce. He wasn't in his office, but the duty officer beeped him for us. He called back less than five minutes later.

"Is it getting any better over there?" he asked.

"I can't say that it is," I told him. "Jerry Barnes was here saying he stopped IRS seizure of the children's estate. I gave him a copy of the receipt for the registered package we sent to the Treasury."

"I know. I just got off the phone," Bruce said. "I thought I might reach you before they did. There's a Sergeant Ross Harris up there in Connecticut, a very clever man. Scottish guy, all wee this and a dram of that. I let him know you'd sent the money to the Treasury. He said he'd already called in the IRS to get some outside pressure on this. He doesn't know you have Jerry Barnes down there. He knew the IRS could move a lot faster and seize everything, not limiting him to a 'dog and pony show'—his words—with courts and search warrants for just the burned money. He even apologized. He's looking for you to send him the original receipt so he has proof you still don't have the cash." Scarf gave me Sergeant Harris's address and suggested I use Federal Express. "And what about Garner? He show up?"

"Yes."

"What was ripped off?"

He couldn't see me shrugging my shoulders. "I can't tell. The only thing I pinned down as missing was a photo album for 1975."

Bruce laughed. "That a good year for them?" he joked.

But it made me put a coincidence together. "It was the year Donald went on an Indian vision quest."

"Great!" Bruce said. "A crook interested in vision quests. Shouldn't be many of those around. I'll get our people on it soon's I get off the phone." He laughed again, a deep chuckle.

"I'll probably find it up at the country house," I told him. "Come on, Bruce, seriously, tell me what I should do now."

Bruce thought for a moment until I asked him if he was still there.

"Sure, baby, I'm here," he said. "Here's what you do. Talk to everybody you know but don't give nobody nothing that they don't already know themselves. You know what I mean?"

"I hear you."

"Then say what I said so I can hear it."

"Don't give nobody nothing that they don't already know themselves."

Bruce chuckled again. "Someday we gonna give you honorable membership in the brotherhood."

"Bruce?" I said. I couldn't help myself.

"Yo?"

"That's a double negative. That means I tell everybody everything, right?"

Bruce laughed. "Don't get smart with me. I'll come over there and kick your ass. I was in Golden Gloves, you know."

At least he had me feeling better.

"And now," Bruce went on. "I got a piece that you can give out as if everybody knows it. There's a story on the crash today in a Hartford paper. The police report says a receipt for $500,000 cash was found in the driver's wallet. Also, that you left the scene with the money.

"But I also have some thing for you you can't tell nobody. The receipt for the half million is from a corporation called East West Imports, Limited, with a Grand Cayman Island bank address. It's countersigned for East West Imports by a John Williams, President. They're tracking it down and I'm tracking it down. I'll bet you it's a deader end than the Cubbies getting in the World Series. But if that don't have the word 'drugs' written all over it, I don't know what does."

After that Bruce signed off. "You need me, you know where to find me."

Chapter 7

QUITE A CROWD SHOWED up for Donald and Joan's memorial service. I'd guess it was close to four hundred people. There was one famous and truly talented actress and a couple of famous but lousy ones. There were also good and bad actors. And a slew of directors, producers, and other film people whom Donald had worked for over the years, editing their films into good products. But the greatest grief was shown by Joan's therapy patients. One, a thirteen-year-old girl, stood in the front row with tears running down her face throughout the service. She seemed to have been left more alone by Joan's death than Joan's own children.

We brought both Jennifer and Dillon to the service. Jennifer was wide-eyed and stoic. I think it gave her a sense of pride rather than grief that so many people showed up to honor her parents. Anne held Dillon on her lap throughout, and he was quiet, suddenly shy from all the attention he was receiving.

Eulogies were given by me, Frederik, and Elaine, and by people in film and psychology who had known Donald or Joan. The whole thing seemed to blow Donald's theory of twenty. He wasn't the kind of guy whose memorial service these people had to attend, and I got the feeling they all came because they admired him. Sure, I felt the same about Joan's friends and colleagues, but in her case it was a much smaller group.

After the service our little group—Donald's family and group of ten, as it were—clustered around Nick and his current motorcycle. Nick had been too close to an incoming Vietcong rocket during the Tet offensive in 1968. He got a full pension because of it, but it had made him 50 percent crazy. He made a living restoring things—houses, antiques, and especially motorcycles. This particular bike was a BMW used by the German army in World War II. And even though it was New Year's Eve, he had ridden the bike down from Otis for the service. He and Elaine were restoring a house about five miles down the road from Donald's.

"Eats gas like a Mack truck," he told us as he revved the engine.

Although, he, Elaine, and Josh sometimes arrived all together on one motorcycle, this time Elaine had brought Josh down in Clark's Dodge pickup. The truck had a large cab with a small jumpseat where kids could ride. The BMW, the Dodge, and Murph and Nan's year-old Ford four-by-four were parked in a row, country vehicles on a New York street.

Bruce Scarf stood at the curb with us. "The preliminary autopsy came in," he told me. "Cause of death appears to be concussions to the back of the head in both cases. Multiple concussions in the case of Donald, but not Joan. That's a little strange. Caused by the rolling convertible I guess. A lab report won't be back for a couple of weeks."

Since he had warned us not to talk about the robbery, Carol and Anne and I had kept it a secret. Everyone knew about the money. Clark's mother had given him a copy of *The Hartford Courant*. The article, using the police report as a source, said the dead driver—Donald—had a receipt in his pocket for $500,000 in cash. And a tow truck driver had testified that he had seen the dead man's brother—me— drive away from the scene with a briefcase of money. The article didn't state that the money was burned to a crisp or provide the details on the receipt that Bruce had told me.

I spent that night going over Donald and Joan's bank statements—they had invested all their meager savings into first buying and then keeping up their share of the Otis house, so there wasn't much in the bank. Certainly never anything like $500,000 or even $5,000. Cash in, cash out. They both believed in living life as they went along rather than saving for retirement. And they were right, weren't they? The will that they had made out in a moment of rationality was submitted for probate. I was executor and the children the beneficiaries. The greatest asset would be the money left from the accident.

On Wednesday, two days after the service, Anne returned in good spirits from the film lab she used for developing. The rushes on her film would be ready the next day. Carol and I said we wanted to see them with her, but Anne said she preferred that only I go. She didn't want a lot of people seeing the errors before she had a chance to edit them out. Carol asked me why I didn't insist on having the complete, unedited film as a record for Donald and Joan's friends and family. But if you know anything about rushes, you know you don't want all those clap sticks and white run-ons and outs to look at. An edited version of the film was fine for me and the children. I trusted Anne to do a great job. Anne and I arranged to meet at the lab on Forty-eighth Street to pick up the film and then on to the New York University editing room to see what she had gotten.

With Anne's permission, I called the whole gang—Frederik, Clark, Elaine, Nick, and even Murph and Nan—to tell them we'd be bringing the rushes up to the Otis house for a Saturday night viewing. Everyone agreed to be there.

We arranged for a teenager from down the street to sit for the children. We met at the lab at five o'clock in the afternoon. Anne picked up the four medium-size canisters of 16mm film—two for the A camera and two for the B camera—and insisted on carrying them herself. It felt good, she said, to have all that visual record in her bag. We should have taken a cab, but instead we walked up to the IRT entrance on Fiftieth Street and then took the train to Christopher Street. The train was crowded with rush-hour travelers going home from work. Anne managed to get a seat at Thirty-fourth Street and I stood beside her.

Generally, during rush hour my antennae are retracted.

I'm not looking for trouble except in the vaguest of ways. It's not like riding the train at one o'clock in the morning after a Saturday night.

Sure, I saw the three teenage guys—two blacks and a white. They'd been right behind us as we entered the station and had pushed onto the train just after us, making a lot of noise and moving with the roll of the train like dancers in a rap video. I admired their fluidity rather than thinking about the danger they might pose.

Anne and I felt happy. We got out of the train with all the other people going to the village. The boys got out ahead of us and pushed slowly through the crowd. We followed them as if they were our blockers and climbed the stairs right behind them, crowded in by other people, coming out on Seventh Avenue.

At the top of the stairs, the three teens in white tennis shoes turned. They were suddenly much bigger. All tall and with nearly identical mushroom haircuts.

"Hey, you got any spare change?" one of them said to me as I came up to the top step.

I looked away from him and then I felt his hand on my coat. He pulled me toward him—he was surprisingly strong—and then pushed back so that I was off-balance. A second kid reached past him and shoved me. I staggered back, falling against the people behind me and we all went down against the banister and the steps like a row of dominoes. Anne was looking at me falling instead of the boys, and the third one—the larger black kid—grabbed the bag with the film canisters out of her hand and disappeared from the entranceway. The one who had shoved me down the stairs swung his fist at Anne, hitting her squarely in the face. People behind me were running away—back down the stairs—as fast as they could and the stairs were cleared so quickly that Anne rolled all the way down, past me and another woman still sprawled against the banister.

I stood there helplessly watching her roll past. She stopped, sat up, and looked at me, blood flowing freely from her nose.

"The film, Jay," she shouted. "See if they drop the film."

I turned from her and ran to the top of the stairs. The three of them had just crossed Seventh Avenue and were running down Christopher Street. A hero, I took off after them. I wasn't thinking. Not at all. I just ran after them as fast as I could. Jogging had paid off—if paid off meant I was catching up with three out-of-shape teenage boys who were all bigger than me. They cut north on Waverly. When I got there they were no longer visible—it was a short block up from Christopher Street to Tenth Street. At Tenth I could see two of them turning in opposite directions back on Seventh Avenue. The one with the film canisters was missing.

Tenth Street has a series of vacant stores at the basement level just a half story below street level. It didn't take me half a minute to figure out that the kid with the film had ducked into one of these lower open foyers and was hiding out there. I slowed to a walk and went toward Greenwich, looking down into each basement area to see if the kid was there. I checked carefully—standing on the sidewalk—behind each fence and the stacks of trashcans.

What I didn't do was watch my back. Near the end of the block, the kid rose up from where he had been hiding in a stairwell, carrying the sack of film canisters. His other hand was in his coat pocket.

"Hey, dude," he said, as if I were his best friend, "what's happening." I was pleased to note that he was still gasping for breath.

At the same moment, another one of the gang—the white kid—grabbed my arms from behind, throwing his arms around me in a bear hug. That's when I saw that the kid facing me had a knife. He ran at me, swinging the knife toward my stomach. I lifted one leg, and using the boy holding me as support, kicked out hard at the knife. I missed and I felt it hit me in the upper thigh at the back of my raised leg. The guy behind me fell back, and as I kicked out a second time, I went sprawling onto the ground. But I'd caught the film bag with my foot with a blow that was hard enough to split the bag. The 16-mm film canisters fell onto the street. Someone down the street was yelling at us now. As one canister rolled toward me, I grabbed it. The other three were picked up by the two kids and they beat it out of there.

I tried to get up to track them—even though there was no hero left in me. But my right leg hurt. I twisted and looked down at the spot. His knife was on the ground, and blood was spreading over the back of my leg.

"Shit!" I said. I clutched the single canister I had saved to my chest. "Shit!" I leaned up against one of the wrought-iron fences, afraid to move or even to bend the leg. Then I started to shake. I could be lying in the street right now with my lifeblood running out of me—just for a couple of reels of fucking film.

A cop car came cruising around the corner from Christopher just then. I waved to it, shouting, and it came to a stop beside me. I saw a strange and bloody face peering out from the backseat. Then I realized I was looking at Anne. I smiled weakly at her and turned so she could see the blood running down my leg. She had been white before, but that turned her into a ghost. I held the canister aloft like the tennis cup they give out at Wimbledon.

The cops had me get in and told me how to hold my leg for the short trip to the St. Vincent's emergency room. Three and a half hours later we emerged—me leaning on Anne for support—to hail a cab home. Anne's face was taped to support her broken nose. My leg was taped tightly where they put the fifteen stitches to close the knife wound. Anne would have black eyes and I would be walking with a very distinct limp for the next few weeks. And the next set of muggers could walk away with everything we had as far as we were concerned.

The saved canister of the film was reel one of the B camera. Anne said it contained the close-up and mood shots of the first half of the dinner party. The B camera generally recorded characters' reactions (in terms of eyes and hands and so on) to what was being said by the main character shot by the A camera. So what we had left now was the detail without the picture story. And for only half the story.

As we waited for a cab, Anne said, "Jay, I have something to tell you."

She didn't look happy, but I couldn't tell whether it was the pain of the nose or what she was going to say.

"Can it wait?" I asked.

She shook her head. "It's about the film."

I waited.

"I have another copy."

I wished I had known that before I had tried to kill myself retrieving her film on the street.

"It's on its way to Los Angeles," she went on. She slid across the seat of the cab that had just pulled up and put one hand up to gingerly touch her nose. She quickly withdrew it. "You remember Larry Hawkins?"

Sure I remembered Larry Hawkins, and she knew I didn't have to say so. Larry had been my competition with Anne. I think if Donald hadn't been my brother, Larry would have won. Sometimes I felt it was Donald Anne wanted to be close to, not me. I made an effort to stop thinking and listen to what Anne had to say.

"Larry moved to L.A." She paused, then stumbled on. "Well, Larry was always one of my best critics in spite of everything else. We talk sometimes. We write. I sent him a copy of the film directly. He said he'd help me put it together."

Anne stopped talking for a moment. Tears rolled down her cheeks. I wished I didn't have to project why she was crying about this. I wished it were just some facts she was telling me—a happy ending—that the film still existed and would still be made into an award-winning thesis for her M.F.A. degree from NYU. I decided to stop playing "what's wrong with this picture" and just ask her where this was leading.

"I don't know, Jay," she said. "I feel very confused by these sudden changes. I want to be as supportive as I can but I want to finish this film and find a career too. Let's just let things work out and see what happens."

That night I slept on the convertible couch in the office and Anne had the bed to herself. Between the pain in my leg and the thoughts I had, I didn't sleep well. I could tell she didn't either.

$\triangledown$

Chapter 8

DILLON WOKE ME UP. It was, of course, during the most sound sleep of the early morning. He climbed up on the couch and sat on my injured leg. God, it hurt. I was good though and resisted saying anything to him. Besides, I needed him at the moment more than he needed me.

"Uncle Jay, come outside with me," Dillon said.

That suited me just fine. If your therapist asks to see you, you go. I got out of bed and found I was able to gingerly stretch the muscles on the bad leg so that I could pull on some trousers. After Dillon and I had some juice, I got him dressed too. And we were off for a walk in the park. I limped along beside Dillon, swinging my game leg as if it were made of wood. He danced around me.

We made it all the way to our favorite bench, but this time the snow had a New York layer of soot on it. Dillon tried to make snowballs again, but the dirty snow just crumbled under his fingers. The pleasant feeling of the previous morning was entirely gone.

"We got big problems today," I told him. "I think Anne wants to go to the West Coast to work on her film. Maybe she won't come back. What am I going to do? Is it worth it to try hard to hold on to her?" I thought about that for a moment very quietly. Dillon looked up at me and slipped his little mitten-covered hand into my bare one.

"You sad, Uncle Jay?" he said looking up at me. Boy, he hit that one right on the nose. What an analyst!

"Yes," I admitted. "Uncle Jay is very sad."

He looked up at me so forlornly that I had to smile. He smiled too. Then he laid his head down in my lap for just a second—enough to give me that I love you feeling. And I felt a whole lot better. These little talks were doing me a world of good.

I got up but did not offer to race him anywhere. Rather I followed lamely along as he held on to one hand and we walked back like a pair of crabs crossing a beach.

Jennifer was eating Rice Krispies alone at the breakfast nook. Carol had already opened the office. Anne had left and placed a note on the hall bookcase. It said that she'd be back the next morning with the rental car to drive up to Otis. She thought it better if we didn't see each other for a day.

That was all right by me, I thought angrily. I had plenty to do. In fact, except for the time I spent on the children, I used the whole day to work with Carol getting ready for the coming tax season. The tax returns always started to flow in earnest the last week in January. Later in the afternoon, when my anger was gone, I thought about Anne and decided that I wanted to see her again very badly.

Saturday morning she was there with the car early, helping to wake the kids, make the breakfast, and pack the weekend clothes.

We weren't a pair of canaries—me with my stiff leg and Anne with two great shiners running out from under the bandage covering her nose. But we could see and move well enough to drive to Otis. It would be the first time at the house since the deaths. Once we reached the countryside, snow lay on all the farms and woodlands making the cold and clear January day seem brighter yet. Anne and I didn't talk about anything much—I was happy to be with her and I think she felt the same way. But my leg hurt and her nose sure looked like it hurt, and Dillon and Jennifer bounced around in the backseat the way kids do. But even they became very quiet as we turned up the driveway. Clark had the house warm for us; it had seemed warm even as we came up the driveway, smoke curling slowly from two of the three chimneys. I could smell the cherry wood burning when I stepped from the car.

As soon as Dillon climbed out of the car he ran expectantly toward the house, his red hair flopping. Jennifer stayed with us and watched him go.

"He thinks Mommy and Daddy are waiting for us in the house. He thinks they're coming back," she said. I knew she was right and it made me want to cry.

Inside, Dillon ran from room to room expecting to encounter Joan or Donald at every turn. He even insisted on Jennifer's accompanying him to the basement. But he didn't see anything.

The children's room was ready—Jennifer's Barbie doll motorhome was all ready to go and Dillon had some of his favorite large Legos in plain view. There were two other bedrooms on the second floor, which were occupied by Clark and Frederik—although Frederik hadn't arrived yet. And Donald and Joan's room was made up for Anne and me. I felt no ghosts. After the house had been gone through, Dillon wanted to go out to examine the barn and shed. It was as if he was certain Donald and Joan would come out if he could just find their hiding place. We all went with him, even Clark. We walked to the barn and then the shed as Dillon ran through them. Then we walked on out to the pond behind the barn. The last time Clark had been here was with Donald and Joan, when, after Anne and I left for the city with Anne's film crew and the children, the others came out here to ice skate. Now the pond was crisscrossed with the marks of skate blades, mostly from that evening.

Anne and I held back from racing onto the ice. But Clark went out with Jennifer and Dillon and they all slid around like a moose and two rabbits. Afterward Dillon seemed happier and we all felt better as we walked—me limping—back to the house and had hot chocolate with marshmallows in front of the living-room fireplace.

Clark never asked us why I was limping and Anne had a nose bandaged and the colors from the blue range of the rainbow spreading around her pale green eyes.

Nothing was said until Frederik, Elaine, and Nick showed up. Frederik's car was loaded with things from Donald and Joan's apartment that could be used in the country house. Nick, Elaine, and Josh arrived on the BMW cycle, all bundled up against the cold.

While the functioning adults unloaded the car, Jennifer instigated a game of tag around the house with Dillon and Josh. The three of them all looked very different. Josh had blue eyes like Nick and a mop of dark hair. Jennifer looked like Joan, with blue eyes and brown curly hair, while Dillon's dark red hair and brown eyes looked like no one else. When they'd had enough of running around, Josh took them all up to the children's room to help him build one of his block tower extravaganzas.

Anne and I waited in our chairs by the fire. I couldn't move anymore and I guess she couldn't either.

"What happened?" Frederik shouted as soon as he saw Anne. Elaine seconded Frederik's question as she and Nick came in right behind him.

Nick just looked at us as if it was the most normal thing in the world. His crazy blue eyes seemed to dart to every corner of the room.

"We got mugged," Anne told them. And she gave them the whole story so that I got my share of sympathy.

They sat down around the fire and Clark went out to make them some hot chocolate with marshmallows. The fire felt warm and good.

"There is a copy," Anne ended by telling them. "There's only one reel here. But a complete duplicate copy was mailed to a friend of mine in California. He's going to help me edit it." Anne glanced nervously in my direction and stopped talking. I'm sure Elaine knew who she was talking about.

Clark came back with the hot chocolate and we sat looking at the fire, not saying much.

"So we're taking a look at the one you saved?" Nick asked.

"I guess it's okay with me," Anne said. "You just have to remember that not only it is unedited, I haven't even seen it myself, and I was going to look at all four reels before we did this."

"We're all professionals here," Frederik said. He had always worked on Donald's film editing teams.

The constant pain in my leg made me tired and I excused myself to go upstairs for a nap. It was close to six-thirty when I woke up. The house was filled with the good smells of cooking foods. Clark prided himself on using his summer herbs and squashes in winter meals.

When I came downstairs—which is harder to do trying to keep one leg stiff than going up—Murph was standing by the fire in the living room with his Scotch in one hand. He grinned at me when I came in, his heavy brown mustache pulling up the corners of his mouth. He pushed his horn-rims up on his nose.

"When did you get here?" I asked him.

"Come on," he said. "You think Nan and I would miss one second of this dinner party. We've got everyone here from the dinner last week." He paused and looked me up and down. He had seen me limping as I came in. "Besides, I hear you're the local hero."

I grinned back at him. "It was a good fight but I was outgunned."

"You okay?" he asked with real concern.

"Yeah," I told him, "and I even saved one can of film."

"So I heard," Murph said. "And that you didn't even have to."

I nodded glumly.

"But it gives us something to look at tonight, thank you," he finished. He went over to the liquor cabinet. He pulled out a second glass, put some ice and Johnnie Walker in it, then refilled his own glass.

"Everyone else cooking?" I asked. I could hear that a bunch of people were in the kitchen.

Murph nodded toward the parlor next door. "Anne's lying down on the couch in there. Frederik bundled up the kids for a walk. They were very excited about going out on the pond in the dark. I think Nan's looking after the pie she brought over. And the rest are also in the kitchen with Clark." He crossed to me and handed me the drink. We clicked our glasses together and Murph said, "Here's looking at you."

It tasted good.

Just then Nick came in from the kitchen.

"How's the BMW?" I asked him.

He grinned at me and squinted his eyes in pleasure at the very idea of the cycle's engine purring away. Murph made him a Scotch too without even asking. Nick took it and gulped it down as if it were water.

"Did you find out where the half million came from?" Nick asked me.

I shook my head.

"You interested in theories?"

"I'll take anything," I said.

"It's my thought that it's something to do with the sixties."

I had to admit I probably looked at Nick as though he were crazy—but he was crazy. Even then he took a look around the room as though we were conspiring on something.

Murph glanced at me and then back at Nick. I could see his ears open up. Murph was always ready to be surprised by us. I was suddenly afraid of what Nick might say and how Murph might misinterpret it. I wouldn't want to put anyone down because of their job or education, but Murph had never aspired to be anything other than a postmaster. He never joined any intellectual argument—and there were plenty of them around Donald and Joan's table. Scotch and dope were obviously his two pleasures in life. In fact, I had the impression that by noon on any given day, Nan was wringing her hands and Murph had had a couple. Perhaps he'd had several Scotches at home today before crossing the street.

But if Nick stumbled on a good theory . . . well, I'd take anything at this point. I couldn't predict what might lead to the truth.

"What do you mean by the sixties, Nick?" I asked. I had lowered myself onto the couch.

"Come on," Nick said and there was a note of frustration in his voice that seemed close to disgust. "You've heard all the stuff they talked about over the years. Everything that was coming down."

Murph had taken a seat too—a little way across the room, as though he didn't want to get too close to Nick for fear it might be catching.

"No, Nick," I said very carefully. "I still don't understand what you're talking about."

Nick's face began to get red and he glanced around the room and took in Murph as if he didn't want any of the others to hear what he was about to say.

"Okay to talk in front of Murph?" he asked me.

I looked over at Murph and he looked right back at me.

"Sure," I said. "I bet Murph joined the IRA in his younger days." I winked at Murph as though we were all having a good time. "Didn't you, Murph?"

Nick's long white hair and wild blue eyes suddenly took on the aspect of insight. When he turned to look at Murph, I could see the scar where he had been sewn up in back of his right ear.

Nick went on. "He talked about being a Weatherman. About the Weather Underground."

"That was in his angry phase," I told him.

"Yeah. And only a couple of years ago a bunch of them tried to rob a bank in Nyack."

"Okay," I said, nodding for him to go on. He was acting as if there was an obvious conclusion I should be jumping to.

"Okay. Say he robbed a bank sometime." Nick gestured in a large circle with an arm. "It could be anytime. It could have been twenty years ago. Yeah, say it was twenty years ago."

I started nodding my head more vigorously just to get him to go on.

"Say he still knew where the money was buried, hidden. Maybe it was under his bed all along."

Nick looked at me to see if I was getting it and I tried to look encouraging. Murph's eyes seemed to have opened to twice their normal size.

"Maybe he never intended to pull the money out. But something scared him. One of the crazy guys or gals from his old group show up or call. What if it scares Donald? What if he decides it's time to take the money and bail out? Maybe he was on his way to Brazil or something. Or what if he just had information that the cops were closing in on solving the robbery?"

I could see how somebody like Nick could devise a huge conspiracy theory after sitting at the dinner table with Donald for a few years. Donald lived a large life. But I thought Nick's idea was a fantasy. Except for one thing about it: there was the $500,000. That seemed to be a fantasy world production too. But there it was.

"Thanks, Nick, it's an idea. I hope not the right one. But like I said, I'll take anything I can get. If you don't mind, I think I'll bring up every theory I've heard at dinner. Maybe it will start somebody thinking about something that will lead to the truth." I shook my head. "I hope it's a more logical explanation than that."

Murph got up and went to fill his glass one more time. He could see that I hadn't finished enough of mine for him to offer more. Noticing him again, Nick jumped at him.

"What do you think of that, Murph?" he asked.

"Why not?" he said, pouring the Scotch over fresh ice. "Indeed, why not."

Frederik and the kids soon came back from their adventure on the ice in the dark. And just as they came in, the cooks declared dinner ready and we moved into the dining room.

Clark had roasted two chickens for us. And Clark's acorn squash baked with brown sugar and maple syrup melted in the mouth. The dressing was made with chestnuts and herbs from the garden. The green beans had also been fresh, frozen from the garden. A Waldorf salad—always the winter favorite—used apples from the supply in the basement. Frederik had already poured a robust red wine for all of us, except the children and Nan, who never drank.

We did not leave Donald and Joan's seats empty. Elaine sat at the head of the table where Donald usually sat. I sat on the other side of Dillon at Joan's place. Two empty chairs were left at the far end—representing Donald and Joan but not at their usual places.

"You know what this is?" Murph said as Clark began carving one of the chickens. We all looked at him.

"What is it, Murph?" Elaine asked. I knew I had seen him drink three Scotches, so God knows how many he had really had. Murph raised his wineglass and everybody except Nan did the same.

"This is a wake. It's a lovely Irish tradition. Let me tell you how it works. We all get a little drunk so we can really get everything we want off our chests about the deceased."

Nick laughed out loud.

"Frank, you've had too much," I heard Nan say quietly to Murph.

Murph turned on her belligerently. "Leave me alone. It's an old Irish tradition. We just don't have the bodies to view. Everything else is the same."

We were all quiet for a moment. Then Elaine spoke.

"I think you're right, Murph," she said in about the quietest voice I'd ever heard her use. "It's time to mourn the dead." She took a small sip from her wineglass and we all did the same. Murph sat back, both vindicated and defused. She turned to me. "What do you think, Jay."

I nodded. "Sure," I said, "I guess it's the truth. It's the first time we've all been together." I gestured toward the children. "We have to have some reason to what we say. We have to emphasize the positive. Donald was a fine brother. I loved Joan too. And I know you each loved them as much as I did, perhaps even more—we are all family here. Donald's group of twenty. You are the people they would have wanted here tonight talking about them.

"A toast," I said, "to my brother and his wife. Not to their death, but to their life. They embraced life every day in a way we all admired." I raised my glass and the others did too, and we touched them together and drank—even the children with their juice and Nan with her water were included.

Then we settled in to do the meal justice almost as if it

was a ritual to adhere to as part of this wake or whatever you wanted to call it.

It was Elaine who said "What have you found out about the money, Jay?"

"I've been given several theories of how they got the money, but so far I can't figure out the truth."

"Tell us what they are," Frederik said.

I took a deep breath. "First, how about a bank robbery. Say Donald or Joan—more likely Donald, in his brief Weather Underground days—robbed a bank for political reasons. The money was stashed away. The whole thing is dead now. He pulls it out of hiding for some—"

Elaine broke in with loud laughter. "Are you kidding?" she said. "No. No. No. There just isn't any way that Donald or Joan or both of them together are going to live in this house, drink all the alcohol, smoke all the dope, and do all the lines we did together and us not know somebody's got half a million in cash stashed somewhere."

Nick stood up. "That was my idea, Elaine," he said, glaring across Josh at her. "It's possible."

"No, Nick," Elaine said, "you're a latecomer to this group. It's not possible. Besides, Nick, who's going to give Donald a receipt for pulling $500,000 of loot out of hiding. What's the next idea, Jay?"

I looked across at Nick. His face was red and he looked like he was holding a lot in, but he said nothing.

"Next is the drug theory. One of them—probably Donald—became the middleman in a drug deal. I say Donald because I know he bought drugs and Joan didn't. He brought some drugs upstate. Or he was delivering some money for drugs to bring upstate. Who knows? Some deal like that. Not his money, just a transfer he found exciting, antiestablishment, and lucrative."

I looked around the table. "If that's the case, why did he call me? Because he knew we had never seen a half a million in cash before? Was it just a crazy gesture?"

Clark was nodding ever so slightly. After all, this was his idea.

"I don't believe that," Frederik said, wagging his black beard back and forth and furrowing his eyes and brows as he so often did. "Donald might do something like that. But he wouldn't include us in the danger of it—using this house and going directly to Jay's house—unless he got our permission and we shared the rewards. He certainly wouldn't have taken the money to Jay's house to show him. He knows Jay's opposed to drugs and although Jay looks the other way when we use them, I'd hate to speculate what he might do if he thought Donald made a living dealing drugs. No, I don't think the drug deal theory makes sense. Donald was too close to Jay to even be dealing, let alone bragging to him about a $500,000 surprise."

"What do you think about the money, then?" I asked Frederik. "You've had some time to think about it."

"What about the money Joan inherited from her uncle last year? Do you know how much it was?" Frederik went on without waiting for me to answer. "I think it was her inheritance, and they had converted every penny they could to cash for some reason. All we have to do is find out the reason. It may be a simple one. Maybe Donald wanted to see what $500,000 in cash looked like all in one place. He was weird and unpredictable in that way. Sure, it's a stupid move. But consistent with Donald and the way he'd do anything for the experience of it."

"Wouldn't Joan stop him?" I asked.

"No," Elaine broke in. "I can see both of them maybe doing something like that. It has an appeal to it."

"The records don't support that kind of transaction," I told them. "Neither Donald nor Joan seemed to have much money left in any account recently. I can't see more than $5,000 in any one place. If it was Joan's money from her uncle, it had either been converted to cash a long time ago or else it came from some account they have kept very, very secret. Maybe Joan's uncle left her a large secret account in Switzerland to avoid U.S. income taxes and estate taxes and—"

Elaine broke in again. "I think it was a simple transfer of funds somebody had asked them to do. Maybe an Israeli was bringing money in from Israel. You know how that works. A package of cash appears someplace and somebody delivers it to somebody else. Nothing illegal in this country if you're an American delivery boy. It's innocent and exciting. Donald would do it and Joan would go along. The receipt fits. The other party has the copy for proof he gave Donald the funds but doesn't want it traceable to him.

"The only thing bad about it," Elaine went on, "is that the people who own the money won't be able to get it back unless they go public. If they are Israelis, for example, they can't go public. They'd go to prison in Israel for exporting currency. Under either the drug theory or the Israeli theory, the owner may never claim it. The owner may not even know part of it still exists."

Elaine stopped speaking and there was a moment of quiet around the table. Clark jumped up.

"Everyone want a piece of Nan's homemade apple pie?" he asked.

There was unanimous approval. The big question for the moment became whether or not the pie was better with cheddar cheese or ice cream. After the orders had been given and Clark returned to the table with the pie, Frederik asked me if I had learned anything new from this discussion.

"Only that it remains a mystery," I said. "But the solution could have horrible tax consequences. If it is income, the children would be left with nothing—not even this house."

"Taxes," Elaine said. "Money. Who gives a shit about that, Jay. Let's talk about something else."

I glared back at her. "The only reason this house is not padlocked today is because Jerry Barnes got a termination assessment against Donald and Joan suspended."

Murph, who had been very quiet since his original outburst, got up and found the brandy as Clark passed around the apple pie. He insisted that we each have some brandy—for the sake of the tradition of his wake. All except Nan joined him as he poured us a shot each and set the bottle in the middle of the table.

Elaine put Donald's favorite piece of music—Neil Young

singing "Helpless"—on the CD player. Donald had once listened to this for three days straight, neither sleeping nor leaving the apartment. And it was before CD's, when he had to move the needle on the album each time the song ended.

Jennifer asked to be excused. Dillon and Josh jumped down to follow her. They disappeared upstairs to continue building a Josh block creation.

Then we moved to the living room to see the film.

Chapter 9

DONALD AND FREDERIK HAD once painted one wall a
reflective white, which made it perfect for showing films.
Frederik got out the old institutional 16-mm Bell & Howell
he'd gotten at a Methodist church rummage sale and set it
up while the rest of us swung the couch and chairs around
to face the projection wall. Anne came in with her one reel
of film, and Clark brought in three chairs from the dining-
room table. Frederik took the film and loaded it into the
projector.

Murph made a trip back to the dining-room table for the
brandy as soon as everyone was settled. He insisted on filling
everyone's glass.

"A wake's no good if you don't drink up," he told Nan very
pointedly.

"Okay," Anne said, "what I have here is the film Jay res-
cued from the muggers. The lab had put together four reels
all together, two for the A camera and two for the B camera.
This is the rush from the first reel of the B camera. It finishes
just before Donald began his story of the vision quest. You
probably know that the A camera carried the storyline or, in
this case, the main shot of a scene. The B cameraman was
to concentrate on anything else of interest away from, or a
small detail of, the main shot." She looked back at Frederik,

who nodded that he was ready to go. "I suppose this reel is about twenty minutes long. And I imagine that it is composed of ten or twelve different cuts, which match the cuts on the A camera."

She looked back at Frederik and said, "Roll it."

Clark flicked the lights and the film began.

Each scene was marked with Anne's grip man who snapped the clap stick markers as he announced the camera and scene.

B Camera, Scene 1: There are two pairs of boots, Elaine's and Josh's, coming in the back door and being stamped to get the snow off.

"Hello," Elaine says.

"Welcome," says Clark. "We've got some great food cooking."

Then Elaine bends down—we see only her army greatcoat from the upper arms down—and unbuckles Josh's boots. Then she unties her own and they each kick them off. Josh's little pair of feet are seen running by as he shouts, "Hi, everybody!"

Scene 2: Three drink glasses sit on the liquor cabinet with ice in them.

"This is more like it," Murph said. "I remember this part well."

I looked around at him as Frederik said, "Leave it alone, Murph."

Someone's hand reaches out with a bottle of Johnnie Walker and pours it into each of the glasses. Water then follows in some. There is laughter and greeting in the background.

"Those are Donald's hands," Elaine said. "God, he had such nice hands."

The glasses are followed as they are carried and given

to Elaine's many-ringed hand and Joan's small hand with the wedding band and diamond on the ring finger.

Scene 3: Joan is watching someone. Her curly brown hair is almost like a ball around her head, and her favorite blue topaz earrings dangle beneath her hair, matching her clear blue eyes.

"I know what you want, Murph," Donald says. "One triple Scotch coming up."

"Ahh!" Murph said.

Joan's face takes on almost a look of pain and then she smiles.

Scene 4: Roast beef, Yorkshire pudding, green beans, mashed potatoes, acorn squash, Bordelaise sauce, Waldorf salad, blue Wedgwood china, real silver sparkling, red linen napkins and tablecloth. Frederik's hand with his long and delicate fingers pours the red wine into clear crystal wineglasses. Clark's hands with a carving knife and fork begin to cut into the roast beef. His fingers are stubby and there is still some dirt under the nails.

"We always have the best food here," Elaine is saying.

Murph is heard responding, "Food. And drink too."

Scene 5: Josh, a mop of black hair and blue eyes, is seen from table level. The camera is shooting him from across the table between Joan and Murph.

"My God, Nan," Murph said, "doesn't Anne have some lovely bit of film here. Look at that." He staggered to his feet and approached the wall where he obliterated the picture with his shadow as he stepped in front of the projector. I was right behind him and I saw the tiny figures out of focus on the back of his shirt.

"Come on, Murph," Elaine shouted. "Sit down. We can't see the picture."

"But it brings back so much," Murph said, on the verge

of becoming a teary-eyed drunk. "There's us having our food and our drink so close together. Just like we were all still alive and carrying on."

Nan got up and grabbed Murph by the elbow and pulled him back away from the screen area so that he almost fell into his chair. The next scene was in progress.

Scene 6: There's Anne's face, green eyes, and long brown hair; then Frederik, black beard and black flashing eyes; then Jennifer with her small face, brown hair bobbed with two "rainbow sprinkle" barrettes, trying to look serious to match the adults and Josh and finally Elaine, red hair held up on top, one earring of gold, the other of onyx, both dangling beneath her hair. They are all listening while she describes her visit to old Mr. Dorton and his decrepit bookstore.

Scene 7: There's my own face, looking good with a full head of brown hair, wide faced, almost intelligent I'd say. Then comes Nan with her dirty-blond hair and pale, washed-out blue eyes and no makeup or jewelry. Nan glances nervously at Murph, who is next. He looks directly into the camera.

"That then, was a very handsome fellow," Murph commented.

Scene 8: Half a platter of roast beef, half a serving dish of mashed potatoes, a child's plate with the food pushed around and some of it on the table. Three wineglasses with three different levels of wine. Elaine's ringed fingers holding a knife and fork cutting the beef in the European way and picking up the piece with the fork in her left hand and transporting it to her mouth.

Scene 9: Donald's face. He is concentrating on Joan, who is heard giving her views on Freud. He looks so happy. Nodding and laughing with all of us. His lips pursed in silent agreement. He nods as he laughs, his bald head catching the light.

I heard something and glanced across the beam of light from the projection to Frederik. Tears were streaming down his face. He looked over at me, dark eyes glistening, and he smiled.

> *Donald is held in portrait for several good beats. He turns his head back and forth to exchange looks with the other people at the table. Then he reaches out and picks up Dillon, who has slipped off of the chair beside him. Dillon smiles happily, showing us both dimples as Donald folds his arms around him and holds him.*

I started to cry. It was Frederik who set me off. But I was as quiet as he was, just some tears I couldn't control running down my face. I lifted up my arm and wiped my cheek with the sleeve.

"Donald, Donald, how we loved ye," Murph said. He looked around at us and I looked with him, trying to hide my tears. But I saw that Clark and Nan and Elaine and Anne cried too.

Murph got to his feet again and approached the screen. Donald's image became a black shadow as Murph stepped between the projector's lens and the picture on the wall.

"Donald, Donald, how we loved ye," Murph repeated, swaying as though he had intended to step through the wall into the picture with Donald.

Frederik rose to his feet. "Murph, you're breaking up the film. Now sit down before—"

Murph turned. "Before what? You think none of the rest of us knew this man? This woman?"

Frederik stepped forward and grabbed Murph by the arm. Somehow the two of them seemed to do a waltz step together, one-two-three, and then they crashed into the projector, sending it and them sprawling. The picture on their clothes spun around the walls of the room once and stopped with a sudden crash and dark silence.

"Are you all right?" Murph said, the first voice I heard in the silence.

There was a pause and then Frederik said yes in an embarrassed quiet voice.

Elaine turned the light on. Murph and Frederik were sitting on the floor beside the projector, their arms around each
other in a mock lovers' embrace. Nick was standing over
them. Anne, Elaine, Nan, Clark, and I just stared at them,
each of us, I think, trying to establish a neutral emotional
territory so that we could go on.

Frederik disengaged himself first. He got to his feet and
then helped Murph up. Murph was obviously a little un-
steady and got into his chair as if the floor were the forward
deck of a fishing trawler.

"Whew!" Murph said. "You guys know more about wakes
than I thought."

I laughed out loud, but Anne looked at me as if I was crazy.
Frederik carefully picked up the projector. The bulb had broken. He didn't have another. It was the end of the film for
the night.

"Come on, Frank," Nan said to Murph, "let's go on home."

"But, Nan," Murph said, his face taking on a stricken look.
"We're here to honor the dead. I don't want to be going yet."

Murph got to his feet unsteadily. He looked around at us
as if hoping for a champion against her. Then he suddenly
started to sing in a quavering baritone voice.

"Oh Danny Boy, the pipes, the pipes are calling . . . "

You might think we would be embarrassed at his drunken
outburst. Instead, we threw our arms around Murph and
around one another so that we were standing in a circle
listening to him sing and even humming with him. After
that there was nothing to do but go quietly up to bed. Murph
went out the door without so much as a whimper about a
nightcap or one last round. Nick, Elaine, and Josh got bundled up for the trip in the BMW. Nick broke out into a broad
smile, looking nearly like Santa Claus instead of a crazy man.

"It's a good thing we got this wake thing over with," he
said.

We all laughed with him.

*   *   *

Donald and Joan's old room was very cozy with the glow of
still-hot embers winking at us from the fireplace. You would
think that with my leg and Anne's nose we would not have
tried to find a way to make love. But if I got into a position
where I didn't have to bend my leg and if I just didn't kiss
Anne anywhere on her face, we could manage it.

Morning was not so pleasant. My mouth tasted as if
someone had come into our room during the night and
dished the dead ashes from the fireplace into it. Murph's
"Danny Boy" was running around inside my head like the
Mormon Tabernacle Choir up close and my leg seemed per-
manently paralyzed.

Anne groaned and rolled over. The room was cold now—
the fire had gone out hours ago. A winter sun peeked in
under the shade on the east window, hit me in the face and
hurt my eyes. I looked at Anne. Her green eyes looked back
at me, showing she felt about like I did. She closed them and
sat up, putting her feet onto the floor.

"Brrr!" she said.

I gritted my teeth while I got my muscles to bend properly.

The kids were in the parlor with bowls of Jetsons cereal
looking at cartoons once I made it down to the main floor.
Elaine and Nick were back, sitting on opposite sides of the
dining-room table with cups of coffee and plates of toast.
They were quiet.

"Anybody else up?" I asked as I limped past them toward
the bathroom.

Elaine shook her head. "You think Clark or Frederik are
ever awake at this time of day?"

I laughed at her. "Not likely," I said.

When I got out of the bathroom, I helped myself to coffee
and popped a couple of English muffins into the toaster.
Then I came back to the table and pulled up a chair. Neither
Nick nor Elaine looked happy and I wondered if I'd walked
into the middle of a fight.

"Damn!" I heard Anne say from the living room.

"Come on and get some coffee," I shouted to her. "You'll
feel a hundred percent better."

She came to the door of the dining room and stood there looking at us as well as around the room.

"Anyone remember where the film was put when we finished last night?"

"I think Frederik left it right there on the coffee table," I said. "Isn't it on the coffee table?"

Anne shook her head.

For the next twenty minutes the four of us looked everywhere we could think of that Frederik might have put the film. Finally I convinced Anne to sit down and have some breakfast. Frederik would know where the film was when he woke up. He might have it under his pillow or something.

We all jumped when we heard Frederik's bedroom door open. He came down the stairs in his black silk Japanese bathrobe on his way to relieve himself before going back to sleep. But Anne cornered him.

Frederik didn't know where the film was either. That was enough for Anne to wake up Clark, presuming he had to know if no one else did. But he didn't. The film was missing.

We sat around the breakfast table with half-filled cups of coffee gone cold, frowning at one another.

Why would one of us hide the film? Who?

"It must be Dillon," Anne finally said. Anne and I brought Dillon out for interrogation. Did he take the film canister? Did he hide it somewhere? But you know how that goes. A two-year-old may or may not have done it and can't remember. In fact, we couldn't be sure he understood what we were asking. Jennifer and Josh claimed they had neither seen the film nor witnessed Dillon carrying it around. But they could have missed him.

When we left on Sunday afternoon, the film was still missing.

$\triangledown$

Chapter 10

ANNE LEFT FOR CALIFORNIA on Monday.

It was a surprise to me. She took Jennifer to school while Carol and I were having a tax season organizational meeting in the front office. Dillon was with us. We talked about taxes for a few minutes.

Anne appeared at the door just as my client was leaving. The bruises around her eyes seemed to be made worse by the miserable look on her face.

"Jay, I need to talk to you," she said. She glanced at Carol, and it was enough to give Carol the hint that she wasn't wanted in the room.

"I'll be back," Carol said jauntily as she left, and we heard her take the stairs two at a time to her duplex on the second floor.

When Anne stepped back to let Carol out the door I could see two suitcases with her blue and white ski jacket lying across them in the hallway. It startled me. I hadn't been ready. I jumped to my feet and then regretted it, quickly grabbing at my leg and falling back into the chair.

"Anne!" I said to her, clutching my leg at the same time.

"I have to go," she said. She came all the way into the room and let herself down into the recliner across from the desk. "I have to go," she repeated, seemingly lost for anything else to say.

"There's never a good time for something like this," she said. "But I've got to work on this film, and I can't do it here. There's too much going on. The kids, the tax business, the unknowns about the deaths—I can't get the job done here." She started to cry.

"I know," I said looking at her and regretting already that she was leaving. I could talk about the children. I could talk about commitment. I could lay a whole bunch of guilt on her. But that would be like trying to put her on a leash. It wouldn't work.

"Look at me," she said. "I'm only twenty-six years old. I'm in the middle of making a film that might give me some professional credentials. How can I get things going if I don't settle down and do it? How can I start a career if I've got two kids? Where does being a de facto if not an actual wife fit into the picture? I don't want to make dinner for you and the kids. I don't mean that I don't want to make my share of the dinners—I just don't want to do it at all. At least not for the next half year."

She was taking me on directly now, no tears. "I've got a copy of the film in California. I've got people there who will help me put it together. I want to go there. Bad things happen to my film here—three reels ripped off, the last one missing."

Larry Hawkins's name had not come up yet. But where else could she be going? Certainly Larry's being in Los Angeles must figure somewhere in this. I began to feel angry. I thought she wasn't being honest with me. She wasn't talking about my being seven years older than she was or about the fact that a guy running a tax business wasn't exactly like a film director living in Los Angeles. She wasn't talking about the attraction she'd felt for Donald.

I thought for a moment that I must look like a storm about to break. A wide midwestern face with teeth clamped tight and lips thin, eyes in a thin line too.

"Please go," I said, "before we both start saying things we can't forgive."

Sometimes people do the right thing in the most strenuous of circumstances. I think I did the right thing then. I held my breath and I was probably counting although I could have never confirmed that later. Anne slowly got to her feet. She walked across the room without looking back, picked up the two suitcases and jacket, and let herself out the front door without any assistance from me. The door closed with a solid final sound. And I was on my feet.

In films, this is where the hero limps to the front door, dragging his leg down the several steps to the street. He gets there just in time for the heroine to see him. She stops the cab and runs to him, throwing her arms around his neck, crying, saying it was a big mistake, how could she ever leave him.

When I got to the front door, Anne was nowhere in sight. There was a Yellow cab turning onto West End Avenue, and I suppose she was in it. I slammed the door as hard as I could.

Dillon heard me and came running down the hallway.

"Are you mad, Uncle Jay?" he said. He had gotten the are-you-this-or-are-you-that structure down pat.

"How about a walk in the park, ol' buddy?" I said.

In spite of my complaining, my leg was much better today. I could swing along at a moderate pace and it was cold enough so that I preferred to stay in motion rather than to sit on our regular park bench. We walked around the Soldiers and Sailors Monument at Eighty-ninth Street. There was nobody there but us.

"What am I going to do, Dillon?" I asked him as I limped and he meandered.

"Go for Chinese food?" he ventured. I think he had learned that Chinese food had positive associations for me. It was a family thing to avoid cooking and have fun together. Perhaps it was a good idea at that. Was he becoming more interventionist in these little therapy sessions?

"Go for Chinese food," I repeated after him and I laughed. I really couldn't help myself.

"Maybe we could get Elaine to come with us too," I said, voicing a sudden thought.

"Josh come too?" Dillon asked.

"Sure, Josh too. Anybody you want, old man, you're the doctor."

Dillon went racing away from me around to the side of the monument that led toward home.

"For dinner," I shouted at him, "not now. For dinner tonight."

Dillon came circling around the monument from behind me and I turned just in time to catch him before he plowed into my legs.

The rest of the day I was in pretty good shape. Every time I started to feel the anger toward Anne build up I pictured Dillon saying, "Go for Chinese food," and a smile would jump from somewhere inside me.

Clark called just after noon. "Anne there?"

I said no, but didn't elaborate.

"Well, you're not going to believe this," Clark said.

I didn't like him saying that. I couldn't believe most of what had happened over these past couple weeks.

"What? Just tell me, what is it?"

"Tell Anne I found the film."

"Where?"

"It had videotapes stacked on it, and it was on top of the VCR under the TV. It looks like Dillon picked it up and put it with the videos where any film should go. Isn't that a riot?"

"It's a riot," I agreed. I got off the phone without ever admitting that maybe I couldn't give Anne the information.

When I called Elaine, she thought Chinese food was a splendid idea. I told her Anne had left for California to put her damn film together and I needed to talk to someone. She said that she, in turn, needed to talk to me. The dinner would be a good thing for both of us. She and Josh would drop by our house at about six-thirty and we'd order in from Empire Szechwan. Nick was up at their country house working on the renovation.

Elaine and Josh arrived at the same time as the delivery. The food was good. When the kids had finished and gone to play, Elaine and I settled down in the office to talk. We brought tea and the bag of fortune cookies with us.

Elaine seemed in a good mood. Of course, compared to me, anybody would be in a good mood. She had her hair pinned back and seemed ready to talk about the usual subjects—art, film, literature, and the meaning of life.

"What happened, Jay. What happened between you and Anne?"

I shrugged. "I don't really know," I said. "It was unexpected. I sort of feel like it was an accident. Another casualty loss. The IRS should allow people to deduct stolen love on their tax returns. Except it would break the country. Nobody would have to pay taxes. Mark me down for a $25,000 casualty loss.

Elaine smiled. "That's a good idea. You know, I always thought taxes were wrong because they never accounted for what was happening in one's spiritual or emotional life. People would get over their emotional losses more easily if they got a tax refund. They'd be more productive. It would be a boon to the whole country."

She had forced me to smile too. "Think of how the IRS would audit it," I said. "Mr. Jasen, can we see the receipts for your being jilted by Anne what's-her-name?"

"You'd have to show them the scars on your heart. It's a great idea. I'll help you compose a letter to your congressman."

I laughed. Elaine still had the capacity to make me feel good.

Elaine then took a very serious turn. "Listen, Jay," she said, "I'm worried about Nick."

We all knew that Nick was a little strange. We assumed his strangeness dated from his war wound.

"What's up?" I said.

"I have a confession to make, Jay," Elaine said. "Now don't get all upset or anything. Donald and Joan are dead. Everything to do with this is over."

I frowned at her. "So what's to confess?"

"Donald and I started in together again," Elaine said.

I was surprised to the point of being dumbfounded. Donald had been Elaine's true love. Other men like Nick were

pale substitutes. But Donald had left Elaine for Joan after
the vision quest. And now he was gone—dead—just as the
love affair with Elaine was revived.

"When?" I asked.

"About six months ago."

She let me roll that around in my tiny brain for a few
moments and then I said, "I want to be absolutely clear on
this. You and Donald were sleeping together—having an
affair—for the past six months?"

She nodded and bit her lip. Her eyes suddenly began to fill
with tears.

"I didn't want to say anything at dinner on Saturday. I
mean, Nick was there and I thought he didn't know. I
thought we were discreet."

I was looking at her and now I felt my head nodding like
one of those little toy birds where the head is on a pivot so
that it goes up and down like a perpetual motion machine.
I waited for her to continue.

"But Nick did know," she said. "He told me after the
funeral that he was glad he didn't have to worry about me
sneaking off to meet Donald anymore. Jay," Elaine said, her
voice going down to almost a whisper. "Do you think Nick
might have killed Donald?"

Elaine was getting more and more surprising. I didn't
know if I wanted her to continue. Nick told stories about
Vietnam. He told about going through villages after the VC.
But the way these stories came out we could always feel both
his absolute horror and his enjoyment of the experience. I
had to control myself so as not to shudder. Nick could do it
if anyone could.

"Wait a second," I heard myself saying. "You and Nick
were together that night."

Elaine was already shaking her head. "I came back to the
city in the Volkswagen that morning. I wanted to come before the storm moved in. The VW is old and small. Josh came
with me."

"Didn't you talk to Nick on the phone or something?"

She was still shaking her head. "Nick loves to ride the

bike in a storm. He takes the BMW and pretends he's a German messenger at the Battle of the Bulge or something. He says it satisfies his sense of adventure. He was out in the storm, Jay."

I let that sink in for a few minutes, moving things around in my mind to make it come out right.

"I don't know," I said. "Say he did something like that because he saw this thing of yours—this lifelong thing—as a threat to his security. Still how does that explain a receipt for $500,000 and the briefcase of burned money? Nick's your husband. You laughed when I suggested that Donald or Joan had that kind of money stashed away because you said you would have known. You were too close. You don't think Nick was involved with them in a scam involving money like that?"

Elaine looked very relieved. "I'm sorry. I got this paranoid feeling. I just had to run it by you. I hate the idea but I feel guilty now, and Nick sometimes frightens me. I think I married him because he represented the unpredictable. Sometimes it's too much even for me."

"I can believe that," I said.

Dillon came running out to see if we had fortune cookies he could take to the others. He was cute; he would break open a cookie himself and pretend to read the fortune. And that way we could never tell what the fortune was.

He took the cookies and turned to go back to his room.

"Wait, Dillon," I said, "aren't you going to read us your fortune?"

He stopped immediately and tore apart one of the cookies, stuffing bits into his mouth. He looked at the little piece of paper and pretended to read.

"Josh sleep over all night," he said. Then he went running off, giggling.

Elaine and I looked at each other.

"Not a bad idea," I said. Elaine was always attractive. Now with Anne gone and Donald gone too . . .

She smiled. "I wish, Jay. I wish."

But we both knew we were kidding. It now had the feel of incest to it. Also, there was Nick. Crazy Nick.

"Elaine, Elaine," I said wistfully. "It seems the only thing I can be certain of is family. Of having two children of my brother's to carry on the blood line."

Elaine looked at me strangely. "What are you talking about?" she said. "Donald never talked about family. It was always his tribe. His group of twenty."

I frowned at her. "I'm just kidding around. I wouldn't love these kids any less if they were just kids off the street— they're so great."

Elaine was still looking at me like I was crazy. "Didn't Donald ever tell you?" she asked.

She was behaving so weirdly that I got nervous. "Tell me? Tell me what?"

"Oh, God," she said, "I guess he wouldn't tell you. You would have to have been his lover for a couple of years."

Elaine became very flushed, her facing turning almost the color of her hair. I had never seen her embarrassed before. She even turned away for just a second, then looked right at me.

"Donald claimed he was sterile. He couldn't have children. I don't think Jennifer and Dillon are his children."

I looked at her stupidly, still trying to comprehend what she was saying.

"Jennifer and Dillon aren't his kids," I repeated after her, dumb with shock.

Just then Dillon came running back into the room, sent by Josh and Jennifer for more fortune cookies. I grabbed him up and held on while he laughed and kicked to get away.

"Let me run away, Jay," he said.

"Never," I said and I practically smothered him with an all-embracing kiss.

$\triangledown$

Chapter 11

I SET DILLON DOWN and gave him a pat. He took the last two fortune cookies and ran off to where Jennifer and Josh were making loud siren noises. I certainly didn't have the stuffing to ask him to read one of his fortunes again. I turned back to Elaine. She still showed the flush of embarrassment.

"Why didn't he tell *you?*" she said more to herself than to me.

"It doesn't matter," I said.

"I'm sure it doesn't matter in your relationship to Jennifer and Dillon," Elaine said. "But I can see the shock in your face. You wish you'd known."

"I wish I'd known," I repeated. "And it doesn't make a difference."

Elaine licked her lips and sat back in her chair.

"How did he know he was sterile?" I asked.

"I don't know. He just said he was. He was tested for some freak reason back in college. It's not the kind of thing that I follow up on," Elaine said. "You know me. I go with the feeling, not with the facts. What mattered was that I was his lover and he had a golden spout—you know, no danger, no worry. It was something I was happy about at the time. I told him I'd keep it secret. But I didn't know he never told you.

88

I never told anyone. That's the promise he got from me and that's the one I kept."

I stood up and paced around the room for a moment trying to get my bearings. Donald and Joan were dead. Anne had left. The children were not the children I thought they were. They weren't even blood relatives anymore! I gave the doorjamb a good kick to see if I could still feel that. Luckily I used my good leg or I might have been laid up another week.

"I'm sorry, Jay," Elaine said.

"Well, who the fuck is the father?" I asked. "Could some guy I have never met pound on the door and drag them out of here someday? Would I have to give them up because I'm not really the uncle? Think, Elaine think! What do I have to do?"

"I don't know what to tell you. I knew about Donald. But when Joan was pregnant with Jennifer, I was still mad at Donald. It wasn't the kind of thing where I'd just walk up and say, 'By the way, who the hell's baby is it anyway?' You know I don't operate that way. I was happy they were having a baby. I suppose I was close enough to them again by the time Dillon came along that I could have asked. But it never seemed appropriate. I thought that they would have volunteered something if they wanted."

I regarded Elaine with disbelief. "You mean that you and Donald were never alone for a minute when you said to him, 'How did you and Joan have children?' "

Elaine was getting upset now and she started to cry. "I wish I had. The relationship between Donald and me was complex—tenuous. In fact, I did bring it up once."

Elaine stopped and looked at me with tear-laden eyes. "He said, 'What you don't know can't hurt you.' His saying that did hurt me at the time."

I finally sat down again, this time at my desk. Just as I did, the sounds of three emergency vehicles came racing down the hallway. Led by Jennifer, the kids crawled into the room, each pushing something that required the noise of a siren. Elaine wiped her eyes and we laughed.

They continued to play on the floor and Elaine and I

watched them for a few minutes. I couldn't help but take a closer look at Jennifer and Dillon. Jennifer with her curly brown hair and blue eyes looked like Joan. And Dillon, brown eyed and red headed. The red hair wasn't like either of them. What man was in them? I felt threatened. Dillon glanced up at me. If I'd been projecting, I would have thought he had read my mind and been frightened. But then he jumped up and brought his firetruck over to my lap and started to run it from my knee up along my thigh on the good leg.

"That's silly, Dillon," Jennifer said. "Fire trucks don't run on people."

Dillon started laughing and took his truck back down on the floor.

"Fire trucks not on people," he told Josh. They all seemed to think it was a riot.

I think Elaine was reconsidering staying the night after she saw how upset I was with the news about Donald. But I was smart enough to know it wasn't a good idea. So after we threw the Chinese food cartons in the trash and cleaned up on some heavenly hash ice cream Josh had selected on their way over, I helped Josh get on his coat and mittens while Elaine did her own, and the three of us bid them good-bye.

I probably don't have to say that I didn't sleep at all well that night. I suddenly uncovered something astounding— Jennifer and Dillon weren't Donald's natural children. I did know that they were Joan's children. I visited her in the hospital after each birth. I had seen her pregnant. But she had never given me a hint that the kids were fathered by anyone other than my brother. Why did they do that to me?

I found myself in front of the refrigerator at about three-thirty staring at a carton of low-fat milk. Before I knew it, I'd poured a big glass of it and dug a fresh bag of chocolate chips out of the secret stash I keep in an upper cupboard. Moments later I was sitting at my desk, putting the semi-sweet chocolate morsels into my mouth and chasing the taste of the melting chocolate with gulps of cold milk. I reached out and thumbed the stack of tax returns I had to work on, but that was the closest I got to work. I walked around the house one time and then tried lying down and closing my eyes. Fat chance.

Why hadn't they told me? Of course the easy answer was that they never thought they would die. Who does? Let alone, that they would die nearly simultaneously in an accident. They were so stupidly optimistic about survival that neither of them ever took the simple precaution of wearing a seat belt. Which, as it turned out, would not have helped them this time.

I had to wake up Dillon the next morning. I was up again about 6:30 A.M. with bags under my eyes. I made coffee, and went to get him after downing two cups. I picked him up and carried him into the kitchen so as not to wake up Jennifer. As I set him up with some Cheerios, he woke up slow but happy. I made the mistake of having another cup of coffee. The coffee still smelled good in the kitchen even though it was hitting the bottom of my stomach like warm liquid lead. I burped. Dillon laughed.

I had been warned that he would wake up crying many mornings because of the loss of his parents. So far that hadn't happened and I was beginning to suspect that this two year old was the one supporting me and I was the one doing all the crying.

We got dressed and went for our walk. It wasn't actually raining outside, but it was the closest thing to rain you could have without it. The sky seemed close down onto the city and I could feel moisture on my lips when I licked them. The streets seemed damp and it felt like spring might break but it was really just fooling.

Dillon really didn't like the idea of this morning's venture but was too polite to suggest we return home. We walked along—me limping but feeling better, holding hands, neither of us saying anything as we crossed along Eighty-eighth Street to Riverside Park. Then it was once around the monument. I swear neither of us said so much as "Tuffy Tugboat."

When we got back, Carol had come downstairs and was standing in the kitchen doorway. She was wearing a white linen blouse, black wool pants, and black pumps. She looked at me quizzically, making me remember that we had a tax business to conduct. The formality of dress—something we strove never to overdo—tipped me off. This morning a new client—a major motion picture star—was due to show up at nine o'clock sharp. We didn't want to blow the account with our usual sloppy jeans and T-shirts. Our unspoken strategy was to get the account, show them how good we really were, and *then* revert to jeans and T-shirts.

Jennifer appeared in the door beside Carol, eating something that looked like the remains of a jelly doughnut.

"Carol got me something to eat," Jennifer said looking innocent.

"I see she did." I raised an eyebrow at Carol. "I suppose she couldn't find the cereal."

Carol pointed to her watch and they both moved back into the kitchen and sat down again at the breakfast nook. I grabbed one more cup of coffee and took it with me into the bathroom so I could sip at it while I showered and changed.

My formal look was similar to Carol's. An open-collared oxford dress shirt, black wool trousers, and black dress shoes. I couldn't do anything about the bags under my eyes. I just had time to get the kids ready—Jennifer did most of that for herself—and I was off with her to school.

When I got back, the movie star and her husband had arrived. They were having coffee with Carol—and Dillon—in the office. I poured myself another cup. We talked about the account, interrupted occasionally by the little guy. But it turned out to be a piece of cake. I could see that the movie star had decided on us because of Dillon, not in spite of him, and we had a deal.

As I was letting them out the door, a small Hispanic woman was just about to lean on the bell. She was a couple of inches under five feet, probably tipped the scales at eighty-five pounds and could have been anywhere between thirty and forty-five. Her black hair came to just off her shoulders and she wore a red wool winter coat that had seen its best days. She looked me over from behind dark-rimmed glasses, finally giving me a tentative smile as if I'd passed some kind of test.

"You Mr. Jasen?" she asked me. She said this with a long
e sound—meester.

I nodded.

"I'm here about the children."

I almost told her that I had expected a man. Instead I
gulped and said, "What?"

"The job taking care of two children. You know. Carol something told my friend Mary who works at the IRS about it. You
have two kids, right?" Her smile disappeared for a moment.
She must have thought she had the wrong Jay Jasen.

"Oh, Carol," I said, recovering quickly. I smiled at her.
"Come in, come in," I said. "We can ask Carol about it right
now."

We'd talked vaguely about getting somebody to help with
the kids. Anne's leaving for California made child care a
much more urgent problem. I knew Mary. She greeted taxpayers to their audit on the seventh floor at the IRS. She had
the eye of a Monte Carlo croupier and could remember a
taxpayer for years. And all she did was ask the taxpayers to
sit down and wait for their auditors while she had the files
pulled. I showed Mary's friend into the office where Carol
was just hanging up the phone.

"Carol, this is a friend of Mary's—you know, the eagle eye
on the seventh floor. She's here about child care." I turned
toward her realizing that I had never gotten a name.

"Julia Lopez," Carol said, smiling broadly.

"Yes, that's me," Julia said brightly.

Carol turned to me. "Remember last week, Jay, when I
had to cover an audit for you? Well, I mentioned to Mary
that your brother and his wife had died and you would be
taking care of their children. She said she had a friend named
Julia Lopez who was great at child care. She thought Julia
would like us and we would like her."

"Where are the kids?" Julia said.

"Jennifer's at school," I said, "but Dillon's playing in the
back."

"Let me just look at him," Julia said. Before we could
answer, she was off for the back room.

I looked at Carol and she looked at me, tossing me a smile and a wave of her blond hair. And then we were crowding through the door in the wake of Julia to get to the back. When we got there, Dillon was already talking to Julia, showing her how if you pressed the large buttons on a panel for the numbers one, two, three, four, and five, Ernie, Bert, Big Bird, Oscar, or Grover would pop up. Then he snapped them down and showed it again. She was smiling at him. She watched him and listened for about five minutes, ignoring us.

She looked up at us then. "It's okay," she said. "You have a very nice child. I'll do it."

What could Carol and I do? Julia made me feel as if I was the one who had applied for the job and that I was lucky to get it. And Mary was a damned good reference. We had only to agree on her salary, her hours (eight-thirty to five, with overtime beyond that), and that she would get vacation and sick pay and have taxes withheld. The taxes withheld part were my contribution to the negotiations.

She left, stating that she would see us promptly at eight-thirty the next morning. She hadn't even taken off her red coat.

$\triangledown$

Chapter 12

THINGS STUMBLED ALONG FOR the next month. I had to
make a court appearance in Connecticut about the removal
of the cash from the scene of the accident. But I got lucky.
I showed my pictures and the judge decided that whatever
value the U.S. Treasury placed on the money was good
enough for the state of Connecticut. And if the IRS could
wait, so would Connecticut.

Sergeant Ross Harris wasn't happy. But he shook my hand
afterwards in the corridor outside. He had tired eyes, a shock
of pure white hair, and wore tweeds, of course. "We've had
the lab report," he confided, "and you'll be happy to hear
there wasn't even a wee bit of carbon granules in the lungs.
They dinna suffer the fire, Mr. Jasen." He clasped me by the
shoulder. "I'm sorry for the trouble I've been to your wee lad
and lass." He nodded to me sagely. "I'm closing up a case
over Hartford way. Then we need to talk. Will that suit you,
Mr. Jasen?"

I said it would and we parted.

I talked to Anne at least once every other day. Her editing
of the film was slow but she seemed pleased with what she
was doing. Almost too pleased I thought sometimes.

Tax returns, tax returns, and more tax returns filled the

time. Poor Jennifer and Dillon were beginning to get upset. Having just lost their parents, they were now having trouble seeing their uncle, because he works all the time. But at least with my office in my home, one or the other of them occasionally broke through the barriers.

On the first Thursday in February, Carol turned to me in the two minutes that neither of us happened to have a client. She had the phone to one ear and was checking a printed tax return at the same time.

"There's a man named Ben Withers on line two," she said. "He has a farm in Connecticut."

"A farm!" I broke in. "We got one journalist with a race horse and a doctor with a prize cow. We don't want any farms. Just tell him that."

"But he—"

"No," I butted in again. "No farms."

Carol waved her hand for attention. She was used to my tax season personality, when I thought there was no question or telephone call that didn't have to do with taxes.

"He's not calling about taxes. It's something about Donald."

I shook my head to free it from tax numbers. "About Donald?"

"Yes, he asked me if this was the number to call for a Donald Jasen. He got the change when he called Donald's number. She held the phone receiver up, waving it like a magic wand over me. "Maybe you should speak to him."

She had put the farmer on hold. I put down everything I was doing, which was three things at once, and picked up the phone.

"Hello," I said.

"Hello, Mr. Jasen?" In just those first three words I knew that this was the kind of man who could drive me mad in the middle of tax season. A man with time to burn.

"Yes, this is Jay Jasen," I said. I was already impatient for the call to be over.

"I was looking for a Donald Jasen," he said after a significant pause and in a slow country drawl.

"I'm sorry," I said. "Donald was my brother. He died in a car accident at the end of the year."

"Oh," he said. I think he was very surprised. "Well I don't know what to do then," he said as if to himself.

"Maybe I could help," I volunteered.

"Well, this is Ben Withers. Maybe you've heard of the Withers farm in Litchfield County? That's up here in Connecticut. We're just across the border from New York and along southern Massachusetts. You ever come up this way, Mr. Jasen?"

"Yes," I said, "I sometimes drive up Route 7 to Otis in Massachusetts. But I don't believe I remember your farm, Mr. Withers."

"Oh," he said and it seemed to take him a minute to get going again.

"Well," he said finally, "let me tell you why I'm calling about your brother."

I wish you would, I wanted to scream over the line, but I contented myself with waiting.

"Yesterday afternoon I went out to do some early plowing in the south forty. Every spring we have to turn up the soil to prepare it for planting up here. That's what I was doing to the south forty yesterday afternoon. I know it's early in the year for that kind of work, but with the break in the weather . . . Well, I had the John Deere down there and I was turning up that soil, getting a lot done. You see, Mr. Jasen, that particular parcel fronts precisely on Route 7 where you and everybody else has to drive if you want to reach Stockbridge or Great Barrington or even Otis, I suppose."

"Yes, yes," I shot in, trying to hurry him along. "I see what you mean." I wished I could grab him by the throat.

"Anyway, as I was coming down a row to where it fronts there on Route 7, right at the end I saw this thing just sitting there shining in the sun. I'll bet you a dime to a dollar I wouldn't have ever seen that piece of metal if I hadn't been there when the sun was shining."

His reasoning sounded impeccable to me. "I suppose not," I mumbled. I started to pull the next file up on my computer.

"So I stopped the John Deere right there at the end of the row and looked down at it. But I had thrown some dirt up on it in the plowing and I couldn't make anything of it. So I left the John Deere idling and climbed down and pulled at this thing and got it up from the dirt."

He paused, and I found I had stopped trying to enter anything. "Well," I said *"what was it?"*

I could feel him smiling at me over the phone, satisfied that he had reached the punch line.

"It was a suitcase, Mr. Jasen. It was one of those little metal suitcases. And it had a tag on it with your brother's name and telephone number."

I felt the air going out of me in surprise. A metal suitcase with my brother's name on it.

"What was in it?" I heard myself ask. My knuckles were now tightening around the receiver. Carol had closed the door to have privacy with her clients, so she couldn't see what was happening.

Mr. Withers actually chuckled at me. "Oh, I wouldn't open someone else's suitcase," he said. "It's not mine, you know."

My mind was running back toward Donald's life and I remember he had a metal suitcase. He had used it to carry valuables, which meant different things to him than to most of us. If $500,000 had been in a regular briefcase, what would he have put in the metal suitcase he used to store valuables?

I tried to speak very carefully to Mr. Withers. I attempted to get neither impatient nor angry.

"Mr. Withers," I said, "I'd like to pick up that suitcase if I could. Let me explain. I have a tax business. I'm very busy this time of year. Perhaps if I said it was like trying to bring in a wheat crop before a storm hit you'd understand better what I mean."

He chuckled again and I nearly lost it. "I know what you mean," he said. "Why, let me tell you a story about the summer of 1977 and the August storm we had then. Why, I remember—"

"I'm sorry to break in," I said, "but I wonder if I could come up on Sunday and see you about the suitcase?"

He stopped and seemed to think about it.

"About what time would that be?" he finally asked.

"Would one o'clock be all right?"

"Let's see," he said, thinking aloud for what he thought was my benefit. "Mrs. Withers and I go on over to the Methodist church about nine-fifteen and we stay over there until after Sunday school, which is about noon."

He thought that over for a minute, and I wondered if he was trying to shoot my whole day.

"I tell you," he finally said, "maybe two o'clock would be a bit better for the missus. Give us a chance to get Sunday dinner out of the way."

"Thank you very much, Mr. Withers," I said. "I've got to go now for my next appointment. I look forward to meeting you and the missus on Sunday." And I simply hung up on him. I don't know what he thought. I turned to my next clients with a smile. I was really happy to see them.

Later—at around ten o'clock that night—I told Carol about the conversation.

"God, Jay," she said after she had mulled it over in her head for a few moments, "how can you wait until Sunday? This is the weirdest piece in this whole sequence. Maybe there's another half-million dollars up there. Maybe more. And not burned up."

I turned to my desk and rapped on my appointment book.

"Yeah," I said, "look at this schedule and tell me now I'm even going to make it on Sunday."

Carol shook her head at me, smiling. "We, Jay, we. I'm going to risk my life with Hertz for this one. I wouldn't miss meeting Mr. Withers and the missus for the world. And I certainly want to be at the opening of Donald's suitcase. You could sell tickets."

We knew the trip would cost us in tax returns that would have to put on extension. But we hoped eleven angry clients would be worth it.

The drive up in the rental turned out to be beautiful. It

was one of those days when the wind drops off to nothing, the sun shines, and the thermometer tries to push past fifty degrees. We thought of spring. Jennifer and Dillon came with us, of course. If they didn't get me on Sundays, I think they would have taken me back to Woolworth's to exchange for A.O.F. (any other father). Even they were so filled with the feeling of spring that they didn't get into the usual territory disputes in the backseat.

Only Carol had a hard time, her knuckles white with grasping at the little handle above the door during the trip. She confessed that this was her first trip out of New York City in a year. Her phobia for traveling in anything closed kept her close to home. She never took a cab or the subway. Sometimes she'd go for a bus if she felt brave. I was surprised when she managed a joke and put both hands in her lap for part of the drive.

By the time we reached the Withers farm up near Falls River, we were all in excellent moods and looking forward to getting out and moving around.

I don't know why I never noticed the Withers farm before. It had a large sign down by the road where a long driveway twisted up around a hill to a big house on top. We drove right up to the back door. A pickup truck, a larger flatbed truck, and a Mercedes SL 190 were parked nearby. We pulled our rental up beside them and got out. About seventeen cats, a collie, and a German shepherd came to greet us. Seven of the cats were kittens and six others had just left kittenhood behind. There wasn't a hostile bone in any of them. Jennifer picked up a stick and the collie and shepherd went running off for it when she threw it, as if they had been waiting for her all their lives.

Then she and Dillon turned toward the kittens, which rubbed against their legs and jumped around on the lawn, tumbling all over one another.

The door to the enclosed back porch opened and a man in his sixties peered out at us. He was dressed in a slate gray suit with a blue tie and a silver tieclip. He had a magnificent head of white hair and wore trifocal glasses.

"Mr. Jasen," he called to me. I waved and he walked out

to us. I could see he was looking at Jennifer and Dillon playing with the kittens.

"It would appear," he said, "that your son and daughter would like to take a kitten home. Why don't you talk it over with the missus," he glanced over at Carol, "and I bet we would let a couple of them go for you."

Carol and I exchanged a smile, which I thought at the time was as close as we would ever get to being a couple.

"Oh, Jay, could we take one each?" Jennifer said. "They're so cute. Please could we take two?"

What was I going to say? I was just rubber-stamping a decision that could not be reversed. Farmer Withers had done us in, but I was as pleased as the kids. Dillon tried to pick up a kitten by the neck and Carol gently showed him how to pick it up properly. It was a long-haired kitten, pure white. Dillon learned quickly and was able to pick it up himself the next time without hurting it. Jennifer was hugging an older kitten with tiger stripes.

"I'll call her Tiger Cat," Jennifer said. "And I promise I'll take care of her every single day. I'll take care of Dillon's kitten too until he's old enough to feed her himself."

Dillon was running around the little long-haired white kitten like he belonged to it.

"Okay, okay," I said. "Dillon gets the white one. You take Tiger Cat."

"Oh, Jay," Jennifer said, running to hug me while still clinging to her kitten, "thank you, thank you. I promise I'll take good care of her."

Dillon was hugging the white kitten carefully. "What's its name?" he asked.

Jennifer looked at the little kitten curled in a white ball in his arms.

"You can call her Snow Ball," she said.

"Snow Ball," Dillon said and laughed, letting the kitten drop to the ground. It immediately rubbed up against his leg and he laughed happily again.

Carol and I exchanged another smile and Ben Withers beamed at us.

I liked him one hundred percent better than I had on the phone.

"Well," he said, "let's walk on down to the milk shed."

We left the two children playing with the kittens and followed Mr. Withers. The milk shed was a low building with mounds of earth on both sides so that it felt cool inside like a cellar except that it was sparkling clean.

Mr. Withers chuckled again as he had on the phone. "The missus is a little paranoid," he said. "She thought there might be drugs in the suitcase and wouldn't let me bring it into the house."

Drugs, I thought. What a very possible idea. Of course it might be drugs. That was the only thing that might have more value than half a million dollars. Mr. Withers was much smarter than I had given him credit for.

"I put it over here behind the milk cans." He gave us a conspiratorial nod. "You see it's just about the same metal surface as my cans." He reached behind the cans and pulled out Donald's suitcase. Mr. Withers hefted it once like a Christmas present whose contents he was trying to guess before opening.

"Feels real light," he said.

He passed it to me and I also held it up to get the feel of it. He was right. It felt like there was almost nothing in it. But I did hear something bumping around loose in there.

Mr. Withers looked at me and his eyes twinkled. "Now I have a favor to ask of you."

"What is it?" I said.

"Well now, the missus and I have been kind of having a disagreement about what might be in that suitcase. When you open it up, could you just call me and tell me what you find?"

"Certainly," I said. "In fact, I'll just open it right now." The suitcase had a little combination lock, and Donald had always told me that he used the same code for his bank cards and combination locks. "Just remember," he had said, "where you get the news—1010 WINS, the all-news station." The combinations and PINs were always 10-10-10.

I twirled the small combination and the suitcase fell open. Mr. Withers, Carol, and I all looked at one another in surprise. Inside was a single videocassette. I picked it up and turned it over. It was unmarked. There was nothing on it to indicate it was anything more than a blank video.

"Well," Ben Withers said, "if that don't beat all."

Chapter 13

ON THE TRIP HOME, the kids played with their kittens in the backseat, and Carol and I kept looking at each other and shaking our heads. The video sat on the small insert in the console between us. Mr. Withers was clever enough to offer us the use of his VCR, but it turned out that the "missus" was watching a Billy Graham special and, as he said, "It's the kind of program she doesn't care to put off." It saved me having to decline his offer. I may have allowed him to see into the suitcase, but I was damned certain that I didn't want him to see what was on that videocassette.

We went straight home and parked the rental in the street, not willing to waste time returning it to Hertz. Jennifer carried Tiger Cat. I carried Snow Ball. Then I went around the corner for cat food and kitty litter. I told Carol that she should modify the apartment for a kitty room. New York apartments never have any convenient place to put kitty litter.

Finally the cats were happy and the kids were happy that the cats were happy. We left them all playing together in their room. Jennifer said she'd keep an eye on Dillon and Snow Ball. Carol waited for me in my bedroom, which also served as the television room. She was punching the play button on the VCR and we sat on the edge of the bed, our undivided attention on the television.

Static. Then a man sat in a chair next to a coffee table with an empty chair across from him in a hotel room. It looked like the setting of a cheap pornographic movie.

I felt myself swallow expectantly. If this was a porno film and people I knew were in it, I didn't want to see it.

The man wore a dark suit with a dark blue tie. He crossed his right ankle onto his left knee and straightened the crease in his trousers. His face was clean shaven and his hair and eyes were a nondescript brown.
He looked directly into the camera.
"All set?" he said.

I gave out a deep sigh. There was sweat on my forehead and I found myself gripping the edge of the bed.

There was a loud knock on the door. The man in the dark suit got up and went to the door. He opened it.
"Hello, Congressman," he said. "My name is John Williams."
The newcomer appeared in the doorway with his back to us, shaking hands. He was saying something that couldn't be heard.

My sigh gave way to some relief. This didn't appear to be anything that would be embarrassing to watch.

The man who had been called Congressman turned toward the camera.

I recognized him. He was Congressman Sam Weitz. I liked him. His district covered part of Manhattan and he was well known as a spokesperson for the environment and for cutting the military budget.

Sam Weitz had silver-rimmed glasses and thin gray

*hair. He was wearing a dark blue pinstripe suit and a
solid green tie.*

*"Mr. Williams, are you the only one here?" Weitz
asked.*

"It's a delicate matter," Williams said.

Carol and I exchanged a glance.

"This should be interesting," Carol said.

I held a finger up indicating she should be quiet.

*Williams gestured toward the chair he had been
sitting in and the camera moved slightly so that Sam
Weitz was seen sitting in the chair with Williams across
from him in the other chair. There was a briefcase on
the table between them.*

"So what is this about?" Weitz asked.

*"I'm just here to take one minute of your time," the
man called Williams said. "What I'm telling you is of
interest to the United States government and also serves
the goals of another government."*

Weitz shrugged.

*"Specifically, I'm here to ask you to consider voting
for a larger oil import quota for Iran. It's the bill coming
up next week—"*

*"You know I'm not in favor of that bill," Weitz
interrupted him.*

"I know that you haven't been," Williams said.

*"And you know it's because I favor countrywide
solutions rather than the quick fix for more oil."*

*Williams was nodding. "Yes, yes. I know all that, but
if I could just take a minute. It's not going to hurt
anyone. It's only one vote and it doesn't necessarily
need to be outside your total strategy. Look, the bill's
going to pass anyway. And the administration wants it.
But my client is nervous."*

*Williams stopped talking for just a second for effect.
Then he reached for the briefcase.*

"He left some papers for you to look at to make his

point. If you could just look at them for a moment.''

Just then a phone rang somewhere in another room—probably the bedroom of the suite.

"Excuse me a moment," Williams said. He had just unsnapped the briefcase. "Take a look. I'll be right back."

Williams walked out of the camera shot and Weitz opened the briefcase. It was on his knees so that the insides couldn't be seen. Williams could be heard in the background setting up an appointment with another person. No name or place was mentioned.

I couldn't see what was in the briefcase.

Weitz closed the briefcase but left it open a crack and set it back on the coffee table. Williams was just returning to the picture.

"You can just take that back to your room to look over," Williams said. "Then let me know what you think."

"What is this?" Weitz said. He stood up and stared straight at Williams.

"Nothing. Nothing," Williams said. "Someone wants support that doesn't mean anything. They just want to be sure. I'm telling you, it's just a tiny deal and nobody, believe me, nobody is hurt by it. You're not even compromised, Congressman."

"I don't think you did your homework," Weitz said very angrily and he turned and left the room, slamming the door behind him.

"Holy shit," Williams said just after the door closed.

Carol started to applaud and me too.

Williams turned toward the camera with a puzzled expression. "Do you think we got anything we can cut up into something?"

The tape went blank. Carol and I let it play at fast forward visual through the remaining sixty minutes but there was nothing else on it. Then we rewound it and watched Williams and Weitz play their little drama one more time. I shut it off.

"As Williams would say, 'Holy shit'!" I had kicked off my shoes and was curled up on the bed. Carol sat in the chair by the dressing table.

"Do you think that was what I think it was?" she asked.

"Tell me," I said.

"That's the briefcase."

"Yeah," I said, "maybe it is. Maybe it was full of money."

"Yes," Carol said, "maybe it was."

I frowned at her. "Even if I could remember what it looked like, it was all burned. It wouldn't be identifiable as *the* briefcase."

"Come on," Carol said, "it makes me nervous to be in your bedroom. It's a funny place to discuss business. Let's go into the office."

She got up and I followed her across the hall into the office. She plopped down into the brown recliner.

"I didn't know you were nervous about my bedroom," I said.

"Come off it, Jay," Carol said. "This is serious. How did that video get into Donald's metal suitcase?"

I shook my head. "I don't know.

"And let's assume that the briefcase we saw was the same briefcase that burned in Donald and Joan's trunk with $500,000 in it. Then how did it get from that motel room into Donald's trunk?"

"Well it must have come with the video. If we can find out how—how Donald got hold of that—we'll know how the money got there."

"It looks something like an Abscam sting. Williams was trying to record Congressman Weitz taking a bribe. Why?"

Carol sat back and was quiet for a moment, as was I. We thought our own thoughts and then we looked at each other and seemed to join them together.

"Why?" I said. "And he didn't take it."

"He didn't take it," Carol repeated.

I jumped up, feeling a shot of pain through my knife wound. But it didn't stop my anger.

"What do you think, Carol? You're very smart, and I'm too close to this damn thing. What do you think is going on?"

"Well, Jay, it's beginning to look worse and worse. I mean, I don't want to say this, but do you think there is a chance Donald and Joan were murdered?"

Elaine had suggested murder. But nothing had really pointed to that. I mean, if there was $500,000 in a car, I would expect it to be missing if someone was murdered. Except for the money, which I knew about only because it wasn't taken, there was no reason I could think of why anyone would murder Donald and Joan.

"Look at it," Carol went on. "How did that metal suitcase with the video in it get into a field about two miles from the accident? It must have been thrown there from a passing car—Donald and Joan's.

"What if the suitcase with the video was in the backseat? And what if the money was in the trunk? Donald and Joan could have dumped the video but they wouldn't be able to get to the money. For some reason, they threw that video out of the car. Maybe because they thought someone was trying to run them off the road. They're both smart and can keep their heads.

"Either Donald or Joan says, 'Let's dump the video. We protect ourselves by dumping the video.' They think it will be safe in the metal suitcase. It's snowing like crazy and the Mustang is sliding and slipping along the road, when some big four-wheel-drive truck comes up alongside and tries to sideswipe them.

"Donald looks over and says, 'My God, it's what's-his-name.' Joan says, 'He wants the tape. Let's dump the tape and we'll be okay. He won't hurt us until he finds out what we've done with the tape.'

"She rolls down the window and takes the metal suitcase with the tape in it and tosses it so that it slides down an embankment and disappears into the snow. They both relax and at the next rise they try to pull over to stop, but the guy chasing them doesn't know the tape is gone. He slams into their rear bumper hard enough to send the Mustang flying off into space, rolling down the steep embankment where later it bursts into flames and somebody spots it burning."

"Murder," I said. "But that doesn't say why. Your explanation doesn't tell us. Why? The congressman didn't take the bribe. The tape proves he's innocent. Why would anybody kill Donald and Joan for a tape that proves someone else is innocent? There's no reason to kill them, Carol. Is there?"

"Unless Williams wanted to get that tape back so bad he'd kill for it. You know," she said, "I think you ought to give Bruce Scarf another call."

I nodded, but Carol wasn't even looking at me. She was reaching for the phone.

$\triangledown$

Chapter 14

BRUCE AND THE KITTENS made it to the front office at about the same time. That was two hours after Carol spoke to him.

"How you feeling?" he said as he came through the door, looming over me.

"Fine, fine, Bruce," I said as he gave me the double shake. Neither of us said anything else as I took his black leather coat and hung it up. Bruce waved mildly to Carol and dropped onto the office couch. His usual bravado was tempered with either exhaustion or doubt. The gold "Debbie" was missing from around his neck. He didn't bother to trim his trouser crease at the knees, and his black cowboy boots had a scuff on one toe.

"How are *you* feeling?" I said rather pointedly after taking this in.

"Holding on. It don't rain but what it pours, you know what I mean?"

"How's Debbie?" Carol said rather more pointedly and, I thought, without much sensitivity.

Bruce suddenly gave out his Cheshire cat smile at her from behind his tinted glasses. "This woman," he said leveling his index finger at her, "shoulda been a cop."

Carol was on her feet then. "Okay, Brucie," she said, "I'll

111

take that as the ultimate compliment from you. I'm getting you a bottle of beer as a reward. The real stuff, not the 'light' shit."

Bruce looked at me. "Yep, she reads minds, Jay. Where'd you get the woman?"

Carol was gone, smiling back over her shoulder at him.

Just then Snow Ball appeared around the corner of the hallway door and raced across the office to jump directly up onto Bruce's slacks just below the knee, digging in her claws.

"Yeow!" Bruce shouted and jumped to his feet. Then he looked down and saw the little white kitten hanging there. This time he laughed. He reached down gently and pulled her up so that the claws disengaged from the material without doing more damage.

"You got a new watchcat here, Jay?"

I laughed. "She gave you a scare."

Jennifer appeared in the doorway next, two of her favorite barrettes holding her curly hair back.

"You guys see Snow Ball?" she asked. "She ran down here someplace."

"Hey, Jennifer," I said, "you know my friend, Bruce?"

I turned to Bruce. "This is Donald and Joan's daughter, Jennifer."

"I'm pleased to meet you, Jennifer," Bruce said. Jennifer held up her little hand to shake and it seemed to be engulfed for a moment by Bruce's large hand.

"That's Dillon's cat you have there," Jennifer said, pointing to Bruce's other hand.

Bruce looked down and saw the kitten as if for the first time. Snow Ball was being held so gently that I could hear her purring all the way across the room.

"Here you go," he said. Jennifer left cradling the kitten like a baby.

Bruce sat down on the couch again just as Carol arrived with beers for us all—two Amstel Lights and a Becks for Bruce. He looked to me before he actually took a swig.

"So what's happening?" he said. "I'll make you a trade. You got some new stuff, I got some too."

"I haven't been able to give you much so far," I said.

"We don't got diddly squat," he agreed. "We got a briefcase full of dollars. We got a dead fellow—your brother—with a receipt for $500,000 in his wallet from East West Imports, Limited. It's as dummy a corporation as you can get, by the way. The Grand Cayman bank account was cleaned out the day after the accident. The bank has an address for John Williams—a vacant lot in Miami. So we don't know why he got the cash or who gave it to him.

"We got a robbery at your brother's apartment, and all you can figure is missing is some jewelry and a photo album from 1975. Then there's the autopsy report. No carbon granules in the lungs. Like you thought, they must have been dead before the fire started. Both dead of concussions.

"Now your turn. Carol said some story about a metal briefcase and a video?"

"Here's the deal, Bruce." I picked up the suitcase from beside my desk. "A farmer Withers called us Thursday. He'd found this thing in a field with Donald's name on it. We went up there today. . . ."

Bruce waved his hand for me to stop and looked over at Carol. He knew about Carol's phobia for travel.

"You telling me you got this girl to go with you?"

Carol smiled sweetly at him. "We're all capable of sacrifices," she said. "There were points at which I even had a good time."

"Go on, man," Bruce said, "this gotta be good!"

"Okay. We went up there today. When we opened the case, we found a videotape inside. On the tape was a film of some guy trying to bribe a congressman. In fact, it was Congressman Sam Weitz."

"They paid him off," Bruce interrupted.

"No, no," I said. "He didn't take the bribe. He turned them down flat."

Bruce looked surprised. He always seemed to think the worst about people. Part of his territory, I suppose.

"You mean you got the tape here?" Bruce said when I was finished. I told him we did. He said he wanted to see it, so the three of us went into the bedroom, Bruce carrying his bottle of beer. He'd hardly touched it. But now he drained it in two gulps while I set up the video. We sat and watched Mr. Williams and Sam Weitz go through their paces again. I was even more proud of Sam turning down the payoff this time.

"Bingo," Bruce said when he heard the man give his name as John Williams. "There's the East West Imports, Limited, president."

Carol and I looked at each other. So obvious we'd both missed it.

The film ran to its end.

"What do you think, Bruce."

He thought about it for a moment. "Yeah," he said finally. "Yeah, I'd say your brother and his wife were very likely murdered. It looks like they dumped this tape. Somebody was chasing them and they dumped the tape. I can see that."

Bruce swung his feet off the bed and stood up.

"What should we do now?" I asked him.

"That's a strange little thing you got on tape there," Bruce said. "It has the M.O. of some of those FBI operations. You know what I mean. The stings. Abscam. Mayor Barry. They hide a camera and take a picture."

Bruce held a hand up to one eye and buzzed it around the room like a camera recording our meeting. He stopped when he got to his empty bottle of Becks on the floor.

"You got more of this stuff?" he asked.

Carol took the bottle from him and disappeared. Bruce leaned over and pressed the rewind button on the VCR and then played it again.

Bruce walked back into my office and I followed him. Carol came in with another beer.

He dropped into the recliner, this time pushing it back until he felt comfortable.

"Well, maybe I should nose around my FBI contacts. That machine of yours good enough to get me a copy of the video?"

"Sure," I said. I left them and set the copy of the video running.

"What's next?" I asked when I came back.

"Why don't you just go see Sam Weitz?" Bruce suggested. "He's the man on hand, so to speak. You being the brother of the man who had the film, you might have the easiest time getting in to see him."

Sometimes, I thought, police procedure was amazing. You just thought of the most obvious thing to do and did it.

"That makes a lot of sense," I said. "I'll call his office tomorrow and see if he's here or in D.C." I'd have to check to see which of the six tax clients I had scheduled I could cancel.

"Make it a priority," Bruce said. "It's the best shot. But first thing, you get a copy to that Scottish cop in Connecticut. Ross Harris is gonna be a real happy man, he sees that video. This is his big break. Nothin' 'wee' about it. Homicide gets everybody real serious."

I said I would, and we were all quiet for a moment, thinking our own thoughts, except that Carol and I were actually waiting for Bruce to come up with something. He got to his feet.

"Take a copy of the tape to Weitz too when you go," he said. "That guy Williams could tell a lot of shit if we could pin him—I'll lay you seven to one on that.

Bruce started moving toward the door.

"You telling me everything, Jay?"

I searched my mind for stuff to tell him. "Anne left for California to work on the film," I said.

"What film?" he shot back.

I told him about the film in the country.

"Sound's like there's nothing there," he said. He waved a last time and was gone.

I went back into the office. Carol was already entering somebody's tax guts onto the computer.

"Why does everything have to happen in tax season?" I asked.

"Why not?" Carol said. She smiled across the room at me. I dug out a stack of tax returns and got to work.

Monday morning came with all the pressure of taxes. Julia was there promptly at eight-thirty when Dillon and Jennifer were just finishing breakfast. She helped them dress and then she and Dillon walked Jennifer to school. I was in the office at eight forty-five and Carol had already been there for half an hour. Mondays it always seemed a million people called. I snuck a call to Weitz's office just before my first appointment at ten o'clock. The congressman was in town. I told his secretary that I had to talk to him personally and that it was about a man named Williams who had tried to bribe him. Then I Fed Ex-ed a copy of the tape to Ross Harris.

The congressman called back when I was fifteen minutes into my appointment.

"Mr. Williams?" he said when he had me on the phone.

I told him that not only wasn't I Mr. Williams but I was a supporter of his and I had accidentally come into possession of a videotape in which Mr. Williams seemed to have tried to bribe him and he had refused. I needed to see him because the video was found at the scene of my brother's death and it might be related. He asked me to come by his midtown office that afternoon at three o'clock.

Sam Weitz was only twenty minutes late for our appointment. He came out of his office to meet me in the sparse waiting room. He was wearing a dark olive green suit and a maroon tie against a white dress shirt. It proved he was on the political fringe.

"Come in, come in," he said, shaking my hand and grabbing one shoulder. "We met two years ago at the fund-raiser Robert Redford gave for me. Tax man, right?"

I was impressed. I hadn't even thought to suggest I'd met him. Being in films, Donald had been invited to the Redford-sponsored event and I had tagged along, donating my hundred bucks in the process. Sam Weitz and I had talked for five minutes about taxes and the need for an expanded child-care credit until universal daycare was available. It was a pet interest of his.

"That's amazing you remember," I said.

He laughed and his eyes crinkled up behind his glasses in a way that made you want to trust him like a kindly grandfather.

"I don't believe in flimflam," he said. "To tell you the truth, I just looked up your name in our file and saw you had given me a hundred bucks at the fund-raiser. Federal election law requires that we get your profession. I did remember speaking to a tax guy at that thing about child-care credits. It had to be you. Not so magical, now, is it?"

"It's almost more impressive dehyped."

He motioned me into his office. It was large but was nearly as sparsely furnished as his waiting room. Several Bank of England chairs faced his desk. The desk itself was a nice cherrywood affair, and he had a black leather swivel chair behind it. Across the room were six leather straight-backed armchairs around a small oak conference table. An American flag hung on a pole beside his desk. There were pictures of him with various people on the wall behind his desk. Jack Kennedy. Robert Redford. Mandela. Gorbachev. Jimmy Carter. Bella Abzug. Some other local pols I recognized but couldn't name, except for District Leader Curtis Arluck.

He motioned for me to sit in one of the Bank of England chairs while he went to sit at his desk.

"Please tell me what this is all about," he said.

I told him about Donald's death and the money I had found in a briefcase at the accident site. And about the second suitcase, which had a video in it. I told him how the video showed him refusing an apparent bribe from a Mr. Williams.

"We couldn't see into that briefcase when you opened it," I said. "I want to know if my brother was murdered. It now appears they might have thrown the suitcase with the video in it from the car before they were run off the road."

Weitz shifted uneasily in his seat. "There was money in the briefcase," he said. The words came out sharp and short. "I never should have even looked into it. I should have told that bum to come by my office with his 'papers.' I just saw there was money and I closed it and left—well, you know what happened if there was a tape."

Weitz sat back, put his hands behind his head, and looked out the window for a moment.

"Who's after me?" he said.

I couldn't help him with that one.

"I'm kind of in a bad place on this," he went on, "although my constituency is solid. The only way they—whoever 'they' are—could get me is from the inside. A damn bribe! What a stupid thing for them to try."

He brought his head around to look at me and he looked very grim. No grandfather now, just an angry man. I could see why he made it as a politician. He made people see in him what he wanted them to see. "Can I get that tape?"

I shrugged. "Why not? I brought along a copy to give you."

"If I release it, the gesture will seem to be self-serving. In fact, those against me will say it was made by my staff." Weitz seemed to be thinking out loud instead of answering my question. "The only thing to do is to find this guy Williams and see where he came from."

I leaned forward and set the tape cassette on his desk. He looked at it and shuddered.

"I can imagine somebody setting that thing there under very different circumstances. Saying, we want you to do such and such or else." He stood up to reach for the tape. "The bastards."

"But you know nothing about Williams? Nothing about how my brother ended up with this tape in a suitcase? Or how it landed in a field a couple of miles from where he died?"

Weitz shook his head. "But, my God, I'm going to find out. This tape is going straight to the FBI today. I want some answers on this thing. If it wasn't one of their own hare-brained schemes, then they may have a renegade or two out there free-lancing."

"Where did you meet Williams?" I asked.

He looked at me and I could see he wondered suddenly if he should be talking to me. For all he knew I had no dead brother and I was perhaps an associate of Mr. Williams.

"If I was with Williams," I told him, "I wouldn't have to ask where the meeting took place."

He chuckled then and became the kindly grandfather

again. "It was the Hilton on Eyck Plaza in Albany. I apologize. This job could make anyone paranoid.

"Let me tell you what happened. I was in Albany with the Democratic congressional delegation from the city. We were being briefed by the governor on strategies for the next upcoming legislative session in Washington. And we were telling him what we needed too. I was staying at the Hilton and just when I got back to my room I got a message that there was an important meeting in Room 732. The guy said it was a foreign affairs matter and he was an aide to one of the other members of our delegation. Dumb me! I sighed and moved on up to Room 732.

"I asked my colleague about it later. He knew nothing of course. I don't know why, but I felt so dumb I didn't tell him what happened. Instead I tried to go back to Room 732, but no one answered. I checked with the desk and they didn't even have a registration for the room. What could I do? I thought people would think I was crazy."

He tapped on the tape cassette. "Now I can make a case with the FBI and everybody else."

"Do what you want," I said, "but I hope it leads back to my brother and his wife and where they got $500,000. And, if their deaths weren't accidental, I hope it proves that too, and points to whoever murdered them."

There was nothing for either of us to say, and the congressman ushered me out of his office. We agreed we would compare notes whenever one of us got something.

When I got back to the office, Carol was just showing out a client. Her next appointment was sitting in the small hall foyer we used as a waiting room. My four-thirty client was also there waiting, but Carol called me into her office and closed the door.

"What happened, Jay?" she asked.

I opened my hands to her. "He seems truly outraged. Also on the defensive because he didn't try to blow any whistles at the time. The bottom line for us is that he knows nothing. He claims he's going to try to find out now."

Carol sighed and moved toward the door to get her client.

"For my money," I concluded, "he was straightforward and honest. We'll have to see if he can give us anything on this."

"Bruce didn't call back yet," she said, "but I think Donald was there. Williams's name is on that receipt."

I reluctantly nodded at her conclusion. Donald must have been there.

I made a mental note to call Bruce that night about my visit with the congressman. We both went to meet our next clients.

Chapter 15

ON WEDNESDAY, BRUCE SCARF CALLED.

"What's happening?" he greeted me.

There was nothing I could tell him.

"Well, what I got," he said, "is nothing on nobody. This Williams dude is an unknown. At least the FBI claims they don't know who the fuck he is. Which means either they don't know or they don't say they know."

"What about the hotel reservation on the room?"

"Nothing there. I mean nothing. Not even a false name or credit card. It's as if the room was empty. Weitz must have called the FBI right after you saw him. They told me he said the meeting took place the afternoon of the day your brother died. That room was an empty that day, set aside for radiator repair."

"You talk to Ross Harris?" I asked him. "He get the video?"

"He's out. Him and his four-man squad been subpoenaed to appear in Hartford. The Warwick–Smith murder trial. Lover shot two-timing boyfriend. Probably gone 'til the end of the month. Then they'll crawl all over you and everybody else."

I had nothing else to ask him.

"I got an idea just now, Jay," Bruce said.

"Tell me."

"Why wait for Ross? Take the Weitz video up to the country place. Show it. Maybe you'll get something out of it."

I held the phone away from my mouth. "Bruce says to show the Weitz video to the others," I told Carol.

"Man's full of good ideas . . . for a Fascist." She said this loud enough so Bruce could hear her.

He chuckled.

"Okay," I said. "I'll take the film up."

"Also, you better dope out a little more information to them. Tell them Donald's receipt came from a Grand Cayman Island bank and it was signed by the Mr. Williams they've just seen. Perhaps that will pop something in someone's mind."

Bruce signed off and I hung up the phone. "You have any last instructions for me when I show this thing?"

A calm smile came over Carol's wide face. "I'm going with you."

It was my turn to smile. "Another trip?" I remembered seeing her white knuckles during the trip to see Ben Withers. "Two times in the same month?"

She continued to smile. I think it was something like the expression of a condemned man accepting fate. "Strange times call for strange actions, Jay. I want to see if anyone breaks when we watch this video."

We worked a short day on Saturday, canceling our last appointments so we'd arrive at the country house by eight, in time for dinner. I bid good-bye to my last client and walked over to the Hertz garage on Seventy-seventh. Then I picked up Carol and the children and we were on our way.

Unfortunately it was one of those miserable February days when cold rain is blowing from one direction and snow is trying to come in from the other. And it didn't get any better as we drove up through Connecticut and finally into Massachusetts. The windshield wipers kept up their swish-swish all the way, making the road just barely visible. Carol wasn't tolerating the ride very well. The weather was making her into a basket case.

I glanced over at her just after we crossed into Connecticut. "I really appreciate this, Carol," I said. "I know it's tough on you. It's great of you, really great."

"Bullshit," she said, but she said it very softly, trying to make a joke out of the whole thing.

The kids and I ended up singing songs to try to calm her down.

We were the last to arrive. It was dark when I pulled into the long curving driveway. The lights were on all over the house, and Dillon and Jennifer piled out and raced toward the light. Clark was standing there to welcome us, with Josh right behind him.

"Come in, guys," Josh said to the kids. "I'm building a big fort upstairs. You can help me."

We came in and dumped our jackets and boots on the storm porch just inside the back door. Then Clark led us into the living room where a blazing fire in the fireplace gave off a cheerful glow. Frederik and Elaine and Nick sat on one side. Murph and Nan were on the other. They had all had a drink or two—just enough to be happy. Even Murph seemed in a reasonable frame of mind. I walked in and set the video on the coffee table in front of the fireplace.

"Here's a strange video," I told them.

Murph said, "I hope this doesn't get us going like the last one did."

Nick picked it up and examined it. "It's untitled," he said.

"It's a video that we think Donald and Joan threw out of the car window before they crashed. It was found in Donald's metal suitcase—the one he used for films—about two miles north of the crash site."

"What's on it, Jay?" Elaine asked.

I shrugged. "I'll let you wait and see. I want to surprise you."

Murph looked at me and then around at all the others. "I don't know if I can stand the wait," he said.

I laughed at him. "It's not that long, Murph," I said. "And I'm starved. Let's eat."

"That's good," Clark said, "because I've got everything ready to go here."

Clark ushered us all to the dining room table at the same
time. I guessed he wasn't taking any chances on Murph
getting too much libation before dinner.

A roast turkey had already been set out. At each place was
a bowl of hot curried pumpkin soup topped with homemade
croutons.

Elaine took Donald's place at the head of the table again.
I took what used to be Joan's seat. The others gathered
around randomly. The two empty chairs that had been there
at the wake were gone. Four crystal candlesticks with lighted
candles provided the light.

Clark carved the turkey as the rest of us spooned up the
pumpkin soup. As usual the food was delicious. So was the
wine Frederik picked out to go with it.

Frederik raised his own wineglass when he had finished
pouring. His eyes flashed in the candlelight.

"Let's have a toast," he said, "to our survival."

"What do you mean?" Elaine said.

"Here. Together. More years. Growing old together."

"Of course," Elaine snapped back, lifting her glass. We all
brought our glasses up—even Nan with her water and the
children with their apple juice.

"To our survival," Clark and Frederik said together.

The crystal and glass clinked softly, sparkling in the flick-
ering light of the candles.

Carol looked around at all of us. "Is this pretty much like
it was at the big dinner party?"

"Yes, a little," Frederik said. "But Donald and Joan were
here too. And Anne. Nothing's the same."

Carol looked around very seriously. "You know I'm like
some wines. I don't travel very well. This is the first time in
the four years Jay and I have worked together that I've come
to this house. I may even decide it was worth the trip. But
especially if we can figure out where a half-million dollars
came from."

"Maybe the video will give us a hint," Elaine said.

We ate quietly after that. The food was too good to ruin
with conversation. Or maybe the others were thinking what

I was thinking. How, indeed, would we survive as a group? So many things had been held together by Donald and Joan. And perhaps the children would have to sell their share of the house to meet a tax bill on a phantom $500,000.

"This," Murph said after a few moments, "is the food of the gods."

"It's very, very good," Elaine said. "How do you always do it, Clark?"

Clark laughed. "I have a pipeline to the gods," he said. We all laughed with him.

After dinner, the kids were sent upstairs to play and we gathered around the VCR in the parlor room. Everyone seemed somewhat on edge, not knowing what I'd be showing them. Murph didn't insist on his after-dinner drink.

I popped the video into the VCR and let it run from beginning to end.

When it was over everyone looked at me and Carol and then at one another.

"What is it, Jay?" Elaine asked.

"I don't know," I said. "I mean it's obviously a video of Sam Weitz refusing a bribe from a Mr. Williams. It appears to be a scam operation. You all saw there was a briefcase containing something. I talked to Sam Weitz. He said it was full of money. He told me it all took place in the Hilton in Albany. Donald and Joan had a briefcase full of money in the trunk of the car. They also apparently jettisoned this video two miles from the scene of the accident. Then there was a receipt in Donald's wallet saying he'd accepted $500,000."

I stopped and let that all sink into everybody's consciousness. Carol continued for me.

"Jay and I think Donald operated that video camera. You see, we found out the receipt in Donald's pocket was signed by a John Williams."

"I was the only one here the day they left," Frederik said. "Joan was here during the day. She said that Donald had to go to Albany. I wasn't feeling well and I was already in bed when he returned from Albany and they left."

Carol turned to Clark. "How about you? Did you hear

them refer to any of this the day of the accident?"

Clark shook his head. "I'd left for my mother's house in Connecticut. I came back after they left. I suppose they must have had the accident as I was driving up from Hartford in my pickup. But I came up Route 8."

Nick was shaking his head too. "I didn't see them after the night of the party. Elaine and Josh and I went home in the VW. Then she and Josh took off for the city in the morning and I worked on the house all day. That night I took the old BMW out to see how it'd handle in the snow." He glanced nervously around at all of us, that crazy gleam in his blue eyes. "I got nothing to add."

Elaine came next. "I took the Volks and drove down to the city early that morning. Josh came with me. That night, I got Josh to sleep at about nine o'clock. The woman next door came over so I could go down to the Film Forum for an Andy Warhol retrospective. It ended at twelve-thirty. I had a drink nearby and didn't get home until nearly two o'clock. Frederik had already left a message about the accident. It was horrible."

"Well, I didn't talk to them either," Murph said, looking around at Nan as if for confirmation. "I did see them leave. Nan went to sleep about ten o'clock and I decided to run into Otis for a quick one. I'd come out onto the porch in the snowstorm when I saw the Mustang coming down your driveway. They turned and went off toward Monterey. I didn't know they were trying to drive back to New York." He stopped for a second. "In fact, at the time," he added frowning, "it looked like Donald alone."

Nan didn't say anything.

I stood up to make my next point. "Maybe they were murdered."

"Murder!" Elaine shouted, jumping up from her seat. The others seemed stunned.

"Any of you borrow the 1975 photo album Donald and Joan had in their apartment?" I asked.

Elaine sat back down in her chair. Everyone looked at me as if I were completely crazy.

"What the fuck," Nick said, "does one of us borrowing a 1975 photo album from Donald and Joan have to do with this shit?"

"Their apartment was robbed," I said calmly, "the day after they died. Except for some jewelry, the only thing missing was the album."

"Hold on a second," Frederik said. "That year Donald and Joan and Clark went on the vision quest."

"Yes," I said.

"Anne's film is about Donald's vision quest," Frederik went on.

"Yes," I said again. And just as he made the next remark, I made the same association in my head.

"Well, you and Anne lost nearly all the film of the dinner party. And that film centered on Donald's story of the vision quest too."

"Coincidence," Clark said.

We all looked at him.

"We all saw that B reel Jay saved from the theft. I was on the vision quest too. And I can tell you there is nothing doing in linking this thing to the vision quest. It's a coincidence. As for your saying the album is missing after the robbery, well there is no way to tell what happened to it. It might be kicking around here for all we know. Because we know that Donald often had it out and showed it around more than any of the others."

I was struck by how badly Clark seemed to want to avoid talking about the vision quest. But he was the only one who was in a position to say whether there might be a relationship between the vision quest and the present.

"Why don't we all sleep on it," I said. "Maybe we'll come up with something by tomorrow."

"Maybe there's no relationship," Carol said. "But I have a suggestion. Why don't you ask Anne to send the complete film, outtakes and all. Maybe something there would give us a clue."

It was a good thought and after we'd broken up, I called Anne. She reluctantly agreed to send the outtakes, too, although she could remember nothing that would be useful to us.

After Murph and Nan, Elaine and Nick and Josh all left, the rest of us went to bed.

I slept in with the kids and let Carol have Donald and Joan's room. The next morning was one of hangovers, not revelations. Early in the afternoon, we drove back to the city.

Chapter 16

THE FOLLOWING WEDNESDAY'S MAIL had one surprise in it.

Carol and I were both working with clients when our mailman knocked on the door. There was an impressive-looking envelope from the Bureau of Engraving and Printing. I opened it after my client had left and inside was a letter advising me of the estimated salvage value of the $500,000.

The letter reported that the U.S. Treasury was able to replace the following identifiable bills of U.S. currency:

628 bills @ $100.00 = $62,800.00
1,524 bills @ $50.00 = $76,200.00
331 bills @ $20.00 = $ 6,620.00

This came to a total of $145,620. There was a form to sign and submit if I wished to accept the evaluation.

Carol was looking over my shoulder at the numbers and let out a low whistle.

"At least you know where you stand, Jay," she said. "One of the variables has been given a value."

I nodded in agreement.

"Worst case," I told Carol, "the kids have to pay taxes on $500,000, but they have at least $145,620 toward the bill."

Donald had a $75,000 life insurance policy. I did a few quick calculations and figured that the kids would be left

with $17,536 in the bank and their half-ownership of the
Otis country house intact. Too bad Joan had never gotten
any life insurance.

Carol shook her head in disbelief. "It just doesn't seem
fair," she said.

"When was the last time you were at a dinner party and
someone was arguing taxes were fair?" I asked her.

"Let me see. . . ." she said, then gave me a wink.

"Besides," I went on, "maybe we can still establish the
best case. The half million isn't income. Ergo, no tax on it.
The $145,620 is all theirs. The life insurance is also theirs.

"But I wish we could also prove the loss occurred on the
day of death instead of the day after. With back taxes as
refunds from the loss carry-back, they'd end up with about
$325,000 in the bank instead of just $17,500."

Carol patted me on the shoulder. "Now you're dreaming,
Jay. The medical report was clear. They didn't die in the fire,
thank God. They were *not* alive the day the money burned."

I picked up a pen and, as executor, signed the form au-
thorizing the issue of a check for $145,620 to the estate of
Donald Jasen. Then I called Federal Express for a pickup.

My next call was to Sergeant Ross Harris. He was still
stuck at the murder trial over in Hartford. But the staff clerk
thought they'd all be back by the next Monday.

Anne's package—four canisters of duplicated unedited
film—arrived, too. And they were film—not video. So Carol
and I had to put off seeing them until we could join the
others at the Otis house on the weekend.

Carol had taken lately to having breakfast—toast and coffee—in my kitchen. It was seven-thirty when she arrived on
Friday as Dillon and I toddled out onto the front stoop and
down the street toward the Soldiers and Sailors Monument,
bent on our morning walk. We both had light jackets on
because the weather had turned almost into spring and the
temperature was already over fifty. The sky was a pure blue,
and Dillon began to bounce along the street as if he were
about to fly. I almost had to run to keep up with him.

Fortunately my leg had healed enough now, although I suppose I had a very slight limp if you looked closely.

We roamed around the monument, neither of us content to sit in this beautiful weather.

"Well, Dillon, what do you think of it all?" I asked him. He paid no attention to me but went racing off after a pigeon, making it fly up onto the balustrade. He hadn't worn a cap and his dark red hair flew up jauntily as he ran.

"Anne's still off in California. I don't know where a half million came from. I don't know how Donald and Joan had a tape of Congressman Weitz."

Dillon came running back to me.

"Darn it, Dillon, who is your daddy?"

That brought him up short. I never thought he even listened to me, let alone took in the information in some personal way. Dillon whirled around and looked up at me.

"Daddy?" he said. "My daddy's here?" He looked around and ran over to where he could see around the curve of the monument. "Daddy!" he shouted.

"Dillon, Dillon," I shouted and ran toward him.

"Daddy! Daddy!" he screamed, running away from me toward the other side. I caught up with him and he was crying.

"Daddy's coming here?" he said and I caught him up in my arms, hugging him to me.

"It's okay, Dillon, I love you. It's going to be okay. I love you."

But he was suddenly inconsolable after all this time. He cried and cried in spite of anything I could say, in spite of its being a beautiful day.

Jay, I thought to myself, you have a lot to learn about children.

I carried him, held close, all the way back across Eighty-eighth Street to the brownstone. When I came in, I set him down in the hallway. It appeared that he was crying for no reason, but I knew better. I knew it wasn't going to be okay again in the way it once had been.

Julia had arrived, but I kept Dillon with me for about an hour that morning and let her take Jennifer to school with-

out taking him along. Luckily, even though I had to answer
a million phone calls, my first client canceled and by the
time the second one arrived, Dillon was laughing and playing
with both Snow Ball and Tiger Cat on the floor of the office,
pulling a long piece of string around on the carpet for them
to follow. He'd look at me and laughed with delight whenever
one of them pounced on the string.

Thank you, Farmer Withers, I thought, for giving us your
cats.

Soon afterward, Julia was able to tempt Dillon, Snow Ball,
and Tiger Cat into the back room to play.

At about one o'clock, Carol saw her client out just as I
was saying good-bye to mine. We were free for lunch at the
same time. I invited her to go to the Greek luncheonette on
the corner. It had a name I could never remember, similar to
a lot of other such luncheonettes. Something like Argos. We
put the machine on to take messages and went out. It felt
good to get away even for a minute.

"What if this money belongs to somebody who tried to
bribe Weitz?" I asked Carol after we had ordered grilled
cheese and tomato sandwiches and Cokes. "What then?"

Carol looked thoughtful for a moment. "I guess if they're
legitimate they put in a claim. Like if it's the FBI or something like that."

"But if they put in a claim," I said, "then they confess
they did it and we know the whole story. Or, more exactly,
Weitz knows the whole story and can hassle the people involved for the rest of his political career."

"Donald must have been operating that video camera," I
said. "He must have gotten the job as a film person. For some
reason, somebody gave him the video and the money to take
away with him. That's what I can't figure out. Unless they
never cared about the money. They wanted him dead so he
couldn't talk."

Carol took a good look at me. "That's a very scary
possibility."

We got off the accident and the money and talked about
various client problems until the sandwiches came.

Then Carol came back to Donald and Joan. "Jay, what are you going to do to satisfy Jerry Barnes and his IRS raiders on Donald and Joan by April fifteenth?"

I grinned at her through a mouthful of sandwich. "Well he did say we could file an extension until the deadline on August fifteenth. I'm just going to file an extension without payment. Funny, isn't it. We're always explaining to our clients that the extension is just for time to file, not to pay. That it's invalid unless ninety percent of the tax is paid with it. We encourage them to pay enough to cover themselves. Now I'm purposely filing an invalid extension."

"What will you do when the penalties come riding in?"

"Use the IRS option, reasonable cause. Good excuses for not paying enough with an extension are always acceptable. Donald and Joan being dead is a great excuse. First, you can only use it once a lifetime. Second, the IRS is hard put to argue against it. Being dead means you can get away with murder at the IRS. I just want to be sure that Jerry and his crew see the extension if they're looking for it."

Except for a faint taste of bacon grease the sandwich was okay.

"I'm sick and tired of taxes," I told Carol.

"Bullshit," Carol said. It made me appreciate that she hadn't used that particular expression much lately. "It's only a few more weeks to go. Tell you what. I'll help you take Jennifer and Dillon to the zoo some Saturday after tax season. That will give you something to look forward to."

The next day, Saturday, was a scheduled break in the tax business. We'd discovered a two-day break in late February helped pace us to the end. And we had packed plenty into it. We'd look at Anne's reels on Saturday afternoon. Afterwards, Carol, Frederik, and I had to be back in the city for the opening of a Flournoy film—Flournoy was a client and friend. I'd leave the kids in the country with Clark and come back for them on Sunday. So, Friday night Carol, Jennifer, Dillon, the cats, and I all piled into a rental and headed for Otis.

"You don't know how much I appreciate this," I said to

Carol. Unfortunately her knuckles were white once more as she clung to the little handle above the passenger door. Night rides seemed to be horrible for her.

"It's Jennifer and Dillon I'm making this sacrifice for," she said. I could see she was sweating. She seemed to close her eyes every time we neared another vehicle.

"I'll try to think of some reward," I said. "Maybe I can find a box of Havana cigars somewhere."

She nodded, tight lipped. "That would be nice."

The four canisters of film were sitting in a satchel in the trunk and Frederik had guaranteed that he had replaced the bulb in the projector and had another one on hand in case he and Murph toppled the projector over again. I had invited everyone over for a Saturday afternoon showing.

Both Dillon and Jennifer were asleep by the time we reached Connecticut. The drive was easy. There was little traffic and it was a clear bright night. Still, under the best conditions, the drive always takes almost three hours. We passed Murph and Nan's house and turned into the long driveway sometime after eleven o'clock. I pulled in next to Clark's old pickup. Clark came out and helped us carry the children and bags into the house. Jennifer woke up for a moment in my arms, then sighed and went back to sleep before I had her in the door. Dillon slept solidly right through the transfer.

Clark invited Carol and me into the living room where he got some brandy out of the liquor cabinet. The only light was a warm fire in the hearth. We sat quietly for a while, just watching the fire. Carol and I were winding down from the tax week. It was good to be someplace distant and quiet. I felt the activity and strain of the last two months begin to drain out of me.

After we had finished our drinks, Carol excused herself to go up to sleep. Clark and I were left alone.

"You feel like a walk, Jay?" Clark asked. "I need to talk."

I practically fell right off my chair. Clark talk? That was such an unheard-of event that I would have driven from New York to San Francisco to be a part of it. A walk was a cheap enough price. "Sounds good," I said. "Let's get our jackets and do it."

We put on our jackets and got our winter boots out for the muddy February soil.

It was bright and cold—not a winter cold but a spring cold, maybe forty degrees. We walked out beyond the barn and stood beside the pond, a surface of water now rather than ice. An open pasture on the other side of the pond allowed us a grand sense of space and made the sky all the more visible.

Clark hadn't said anything at all yet. We just stood there for a few minutes, looking up at the sky.

"This night must be very much like those nights with Painted River in Vermont," I said. "Do you think of that when you see stars like this? Do you look for the Pleiades every time it's like this?"

Clark looked away from the sky. His big form seemed like a huge teddy bear. "Shit," he said.

He said it with an undertone that made the expletive into a deep sigh.

He needed urging so I asked, "What does that mean?"

"That vision quest, it wasn't the same for me. It turned out to be the most horrible experience of my life."

"What?" I said. I was glad we were standing in the dark. My chin must have hit my knees I was so shocked. Donald had always talked about the vision quest as a key to building his consciousness. I had always assumed that Clark had felt the same about it. Good old Clark. Big, solid, silent. Donald's disciple if anybody was. I found I was shaking with this revelation. I was afraid of what he might say next. I wanted to start back toward the house.

Clark walked away from me toward the edge of the pond. I followed until he had to stop at the water. The water was absolutely still, and we could look down at the stars reflected there.

"I got sick," Clark said. "I stood in that fucking hole I dug all night and all day and the second night I got good and sick."

Clark kicked at the soft earth once, and some grass, stones, and mud splashed into the pond, rippling the stars. The noise was large in the absolute quiet around us.

"I'd sneaked in some grass—hash actually. It really made me sick with nothing on my stomach."

"It's okay," I told him, "anybody could have gotten sick."

He turned to me then, angry. I don't think I had ever seen Clark angry before.

"Would you shut the fuck up, Jay. I'm trying to tell you something. Yeah, the second night on the quest, I got violently ill. I mean I just puked my guts out. Believe me when I say guts, because I certainly had nothing in my stomach that was going to come out. Watch the Pleiades! Jay, I just lay there half in and half out of my stupid hole with my hands over my face hoping I would die."

"I'm sorry," I said.

"Shit, I haven't told you anything yet. It must have been sometime after midnight. I got scared. I just got real scared. Paranoid. I didn't want to die in that hole that night. So I crawled away from it—I couldn't even walk—I crawled on my hands and knees. I don't know what direction I went, but I crawled away from that hole in the ground. I got some distance away and then I passed out.

"I can't tell you how long I was out, but eventually I came to. I guess I had slept because I felt a little better. But I couldn't move. Some animal sense kept me very, very still curled up in a fetal position as I found myself.

"I realized then that something had woken me. I listened carefully. It seemed to be the noise of some animal. I cautiously shifted my position and rolled in the direction the noise was coming from. Then I recognized the sound. It was a woman gasping in the throes of lovemaking.

" 'What the hell,' I thought. 'What's going on?'

"After I shifted to the new position, I was facing a fallen log. I raised myself quietly so that I could see over it. There was a clearing in the woods beyond the log and on the other side just about six feet away was a man and he was quite naked and he was in the middle of pumping himself into a woman. It could have been a couple of dogs. There was enough starlight and they were so close to where I lay that I could see the side of the man's face clearly. He was painted with Cherokee war paint. It was Snow Man."

Clark turned away from me again. He walked several steps along the pond.

"I felt like such a fool. There's Snow Man fucking the brains out of some woman and I'm fast asleep just a couple of yards away. I was so embarrassed I just put my head back down and shut up. Some vision quest, hey? Some vision, shit.

"Then the woman starts talking to him. And you know what?"

I shook my head, forgetting that Clark couldn't see me. "No," I said quietly.

"I recognize the woman's voice," he went on. "It's Joan. It's Joan! Jesus, Jay, I felt so betrayed. Does that seem funny to you?"

I didn't know what to say. Clark was telling me so much here that I couldn't assimilate it. I didn't know if he was telling me the truth. On the other hand, he was so upset and disturbed that this could hardly be a fabrication.

"I'm surprised," I told him. "You never said anything."

"Donald *believed* in that vision quest. He saw stuff. Things happened to him. I know he never knew what Joan was doing while he was sitting in his stupid hole in the ground groping around for the spiritual experience of a lifetime."

"But they weren't a couple then," I said.

"Fuck," Clark said. "I know that. But we were together. Joan, Donald, me. I had to lie there until the dawn started to break, while Joan and Snow Man went at it like rabbits. I felt myself getting sick again. But I held it in somehow. I just couldn't stand the idea of being discovered. The more I listened to them, the worse I felt about being seen. I kept my head down and my mouth closed."

"But wasn't that the time for what you guys called free love?" I asked him. "Couldn't Joan do anything she wanted to do?"

"You mean fuck that fake Indian! Come on, Jay. You know there was a social contract back then too. She was giving us away, as well as herself. She lied to us. We were no longer part of the same commune when she did that.

"It began to get light and they walked away together through the woods holding on to each other. I found I was trembling, shaking like a leaf. I found my way back to my hole and I stayed in it for the next twenty-four hours. I did a lot of thinking then and I had a lot of anger and fear and I shook all over for hours on end."

It seemed to me that Clark was attributing too much to this event. So Joan had taken a yearning for the fake Indian. So Snow Man had gone after her too. They were young. It was the end of the sixties.

"She never said anything about it to you," I said.

"And I wasn't about to bring it up to her. Or to Donald."

He stopped talking and stood there by the pond. I reached out to put my hand on his shoulder. He was shaking all over.

"I have something else to confess to you."

"What's that?"

"I really loved her."

Clark had startled me again. "You mean you had a relationship with her?" I asked. Maybe I had found the father of Joan's kids.

"No. I knew she wouldn't have me. It was always from a distance. Always as a worshiper and friend. Never recognized for passion. I don't think anyone knew how much I loved her. I kept it to myself. But now I had to tell someone. That's why I'm talking to you. I loved her and I can hardly watch all this crap about the vision quest."

We stood together there by the pond. I could think of nothing to say—Clark had said it all.

"Did Painted River let that sort of stuff go on?"

Clark gave a laugh that sounded dry and sick. "He was off in the clouds somewhere. Painted River had a hard time telling if it was night or day as far as our reality went. He knew the ritual stuff backward and forward but we could have been cows for all he kept track of us.

"I don't mean to imply that he wasn't tuned in to who was having a vision quest and who wasn't. He knew that. But if you had told him Snow Man had been fucking the woman initiate all night long, he wouldn't have believed you."

"And Joan didn't keep up the relationship? It was a one-time thing?" I asked him.

"She didn't have the choice. They were out of there the same day as the end of the vision quest. But I'll tell you how much of a fake Indian that Snow Man was. Painted River got sent to prison for dealing drugs—the acid he used for his ceremonies—and the principal witness against him was Snow Man."

I looked sharply at Clark. "How'd you know something like that?"

"A couple of years ago I went back to the Maple Tree Farm commune for a visit. Someone there told me. I never told your brother, though. Or Joan. I think they wouldn't have wanted to hear it. Snow Man was a guy whose real name was Addison. He testified against Painted River and a whole bunch of other people across the country. Then he disappeared. What they said up there is that there are some other drug people who want to find him. Nothing to do with Painted River."

It was my turn to shudder. "Come on," I said to Clark, "let's go in. I think I'm getting cold." I paused as I turned away from the pond. "And I don't think I want to hear anything more tonight about the real vision quest. I liked the story the way it was."

"I'm sorry, Jay," Clark said, tagging along behind me like a pet buffalo. "Wait."

I stopped.

"It was true about the eagle wing. When Painted River swept it over me, it made me feel clean and cured. He had powerful stuff. Just me and Joan weren't part of it. I'm glad I told you."

"You had to tell someone," I said. "You should have talked about this stuff a long time ago. You've just been sitting on it too long. Now it's too late to deal with it. They're dead,

Clark, so it doesn't matter anymore. Forgive them. Forget
it."

I turned again to go.

Clark grabbed me by my jacket and twisted me around.
"Sometimes, Jay," he said, "you really remind me of your
brother."

I took it as a compliment and turned to continue toward
the house. Clark followed. As we came around the barn,
Frederik's Toyota turned up the driveway and the lights
blinded us as it came up beside my rental and stopped. Frederik got out and waited for us.

"You guys are wandering around out here late," he commented.

We said nothing. Clark reached into a pocket of his jacket
and pulled out a rolled reefer. He lit it with a match as we
stood there together not saying anything. Then he inhaled
on it and passed it over to Frederik who did the same.
Frederik held it up to me. And I took it. I felt like there was
something happening there among us that went beyond my
feelings against drugs. We were in sacred communion although I couldn't understand how we'd come to that. My
eyes gradually adjusted after the bright headlights so that I
saw the stars again and we stood there and smelled the
smoke from our chimney and listened to the deep night quiet
of a coming spring. After a few minutes we walked together
to the house.

$\triangledown$

Chapter 17

WHEN I OPENED MY eyes, I could smell bacon and eggs cooking in the kitchen. And if I listened closely, I could hear the sizzle of the bacon in the frying pan. Jennifer and Dillon's beds were empty. I glanced at my watch and saw that I had slept past nine o'clock. It felt good. I stretched and thought about the stuff Clark had told me the night before. It seemed less important by the light of day. So Joan had somehow gotten involved with the Snow Man. People had strange attractions. Why not Joan? It was so long ago. It seemed to me in the morning light that Clark was the one out of line. Why was he so obsessed with this for fifteen years? Why couldn't he have let it go? Maybe Joan made a mistake. Then again maybe she didn't. Maybe Snow Man was just her cup of tea and it was too bad that Clark could never accept that. She certainly didn't know he would be watching her that night.

I got out of bed, tossed off my pajamas, and pulled on some Levi's and a blue plaid flannel shirt. Then I went down to investigate what was happening for breakfast.

Clark was watching an omelet of cheese and tomatoes puff up, while Carol was tending a separate pan of bacon, which still gave off that nice sizzle that had sounded so good from my bedroom.

141

I helped by setting the table. Jennifer wanted to have an omelet with us, except she told me to please dig the tomatoes out of hers. Dillon wanted milk on Jetsons cereal. I let them take their breakfast into the parlor to watch cartoons, but Jennifer chose to stay and eat with us.

After breakfast, I did the dishes, since I was the one who hadn't cooked. Then I relaxed with a novel I'd brought from the city as part of my campaign to forget about the tax season for a day. I sat in front of the fireplace in one of the armchairs, stretched out, occasionally stirring up the fire to get some flame.

Around noon, I heard Frederik rustling around in the kitchen, and I laid down my book and went out to join him. He was putting together a spinach salad. As I stood there asking him about the most recent film he was editing, Elaine arrived with Josh in tow, who quickly disappeared into the television room with the other kids while Elaine and I watched Frederik. Murph and Nan arrived just as we were serving ourselves the salad, but they had already eaten. Murph had had to work at the post office that morning and he seemed very sober. He and Nan pulled chairs up to the table to talk to us while we had lunch. Murph did accept a beer.

After lunch, Nan came over to me. "I really don't want to see this film stuff," she said. "I don't think I can help you with anything."

"Sure, Nan," I said. "This is just a look at the rough footage to see if any of us can find out where Donald went the next day. I can't guarantee it won't be boring for us too."

She looked at me like a Sunday school teacher, serious and contrite. "I'll take the children over to my place with me," she said.

I had to think about that one for a moment. "Okay," I said, "why don't you take Dillon and Josh. I think I'd like Jennifer to see the film. She hasn't seen any of it yet." I thought about that some more. "Yes, I think she's ready for it."

Nan went around and collected the kids. Neither Josh nor Dillon wanted to go with her. But the temperature outside had risen to nearly sixty degrees. Elaine told them they could take the cats with them and play outside. Nan scooped up Tiger Cat and Snow Ball and the two boys followed her out the door. I watched from the window as they ran from side to side going down the driveway toward Murph and Nan's house.

Frederik was already setting up the projector and threading the first of the two A reels. Jennifer watched him and he showed her how the film went through its series of loops from one reel to the other.

Jennifer was excited about seeing the film. "I'm going to see my real mom and dad, right Jay?"

"Yes, and yourself and Dillon and me and Anne and everyone."

At last we were ready and we all found seats in the armchairs or on the couch. Jennifer sat on the floor.

Frederik started the projector and Anne's assistant clapped the sticks marking the beginning of the first scene. I don't think any of us minded seeing ourselves if the truth be known. Jennifer kept giving off little squeals of delight. She was very, very happy to see her mother and father again in this intimate way. And there were little vignettes I'm sure Anne would leave on the cutting-room floor for her *Dinner* film.

The end of the two A reels came suddenly with no feeling of conclusion. I know I had a feeling of let down.

"Did you like that, Jennifer?" Elaine asked her.

"Yes, it was fun," Jennifer said. "I liked seeing Mom and Dad. And me and Dillon too."

"I didn't see anything that tells us how Donald got involved in the Weitz thing," I said. "How about the rest of you?"

No one had anything to say.

Murph spoke up then. "Anybody else in favor of skipping the first B camera reel? We already saw it once. I mean at the wake."

"It's okay with me if we skip it," I said. "Carol and Jennifer haven't seen it but they'll have plenty of time later."

Everyone agreed and Frederik let Jennifer string the second B camera reel into the projector.

He started it rolling and we watched carefully. But it told us nothing new.

When it came to an end, I walked to the window closest to me and pulled down the blanket to let in the bright sunshine from the springlike day outside. It flooded the room and everyone shaded their eyes as they adjusted to the brightness. I looked down the long lawn and the driveway and across to Murph and Nan's house.

I laughed. "Would you look at that," I said.

Elaine, Clark, and Murph came to look out at what had made me laugh.

Down across the lawn, Josh was trailing something long and feathered behind him. And chasing along behind him were Snow Ball and Tiger Cat, acting like puppies instead of cats. Running after the feathered thing, they jumped and played and tumbled. Behind them, running, stopping, walking, laughing, came Dillon.

I laughed again. "It looks like the parade from *Peter and the Wolf*," I said. Elaine laughed with me. We both became nearly hysterical, the kids were so funny.

Just then, Nan came running out of the house, shouting. We heard her voice but not her words. She ran up to Josh and grabbed the feathered thing right out of his hands. As she picked it up, Snow Ball made one last leap and caught hold, hanging from the end as Nan tried to pick it up. She gave it a shake but Snow Ball seemed glued to it.

Elaine and I couldn't stop laughing. Finally, Snow Ball was hanging by one paw and then dropped down onto the lawn. Nan took Dillon by one hand and Josh followed as they went back to the house. Nan had the thing, which looked a lot like a big bird's wing, over her shoulder as she went. Snow Ball and Tiger Cat sheepishly followed.

Still laughing, I turned around to Murph. "Did you see Snow Ball do her 'hang in there, baby,' routine? What is that thing, Murph?"

I stopped laughing. Neither Murph nor Clark had even a

trace of a smile on their face. "Come on, it's funny," I said.

"Nan's going to be upset," Murph said. "That's some souvenir she's kept from her college days. She's not going to be happy when I get home."

Clark turned around and walked out of the room. He said something about Snow Ball under his breath, but I didn't catch it, and Murph watched him go.

"It was funny, I have to admit. It was worth it." He laughed then. "She should just give that old thing to the kids to use to play with the cats."

Elaine and I looked at each other. We couldn't take Murph and Clark seriously.

I followed Clark out to the kitchen. He was just opening a beer for himself. Although he might smoke dope, he generally didn't drink beer.

"What's up, Clark?" I asked him. "Why didn't you think it was funny?"

He shook his head. "It was funny," he said. "It just made me think of something."

That was all he said and I didn't push him.

Later that afternoon, Carol and I had to leave for the Flournoy film opening in the city. Jennifer and Dillon had no problem staying with Clark. The Otis house had always been a second home to them. And Elaine had promised that Josh could come over to play too. The kids were like the Three Musketeers together. Clark was already planning games to play and food they would all like to eat. If I was the father, he wanted very badly to be the favorite uncle.

They all came out to wave good-bye as Carol and I pulled out. Frederik had left earlier (also to go to the premiere) and Elaine had taken Josh back to their country house.

The drive back to the city was almost as easy as the ride out on Friday evening. I pulled up in front of the Eighty-eighth Street brownstone at about six-fifteen, giving Carol and myself time to change and get down to the East Village for the opening.

There was a message from Nan on my answering machine. "Jay," she said, "can you give me a call as soon as you get this message."

I called immediately.

"What's up?" I asked when Nan answered the phone.

"Listen, Jay," she said. "Jennifer just brought Dillon over here. They're here now, so you don't need to worry about them."

"Worry about them," I said. "Why should I worry? Where's Clark?"

"That's just it," Nan said. "Clark drove off in his pickup just before dark. Jennifer didn't know where he was going. He hasn't come back.

"That's very strange," I said.

"He'll probably be back soon," Nan said. "I just thought you'd like to know in case you tried to call."

"Yeah, I sure do," I said. "Thanks for calling, Nan." I told her I'd give her a call when I got to the theater.

I called her back an hour later.

"I'm sorry, Jay," she said. "Clark hasn't come back. Jennifer is very upset."

I asked to speak to Jennifer and she came on the phone.

"Hi, Jennifer," I said, "it's your new father calling."

"Please come back," she said. "Clark is gone and I don't know where he is. Me and Dillon are scared."

She started to cry. Of course I told her I'd be there as fast as I could. Then I spoke to Nan again and told her I was driving up immediately.

I hung up and sought out Carol in the crowd. I told her what had happened and that I had to leave. She offered to come with me, but I told her to stay and tell our client I couldn't be there but I'd see the film later.

I hardly remember that drive up to Massachusetts. What the hell had happened to Clark? Why would he take off and not tell Jennifer where he was going and not call and not come back? I'm a conservative driver, but for as long as I was on the highway I had the cruise control on eighty-five miles an hour. In fact, I was in Otis in record time, and that was from the East Village.

The lights were all on at Murph and Nan's house, but our house across the street was dark. I pulled onto the grass in front of their house. Jennifer, Dillon, and Nan met me at the door. Murph was sitting in the background, watching something on television.

Jennifer and Dillon gave me big hugs around my legs.

"We still haven't heard a word from Clark," Nan said.

I bent down and let the kids get all over me to give them a solid feeling of reassurance.

"Maybe his truck broke down on some back road," Murph shouted at us from his chair. He got up and came to the door too. I stood up and we looked into one another's eyes and could all feel that something had happened.

"Come on, kids, get your coats," I said. Dillon brought his to me, and I put it on him. They ran out to the car ahead of me and climbed in.

"Thank you," I told Nan, "for watching my children."

Nan shook her head to say it was nothing. "I just hope everything is okay with Clark," she said. She closed the door but left the porch light on until I backed out onto the street and turned up the driveway to our house.

$\triangledown$

Chapter 18

I WANTED TO CALM down the kids before they went to bed, but it started out badly. The back door was unlocked, which was the custom there in the country. Dillon opened it and they ran in ahead of me.

A series of pans clattered to the floor in the kitchen. Both kids flinched back and Dillon gave a little scream of fear as they turned to me.

"Hello, Clark?" I shouted quickly trying to push down my own panic. I reached around the door and flicked on the hall light. Snow Ball and Tiger Cat turned the corner coming from the kitchen, both in the light.

"It's just the cats," I laughed. The children laughed nervously with me. Then they followed me as I went from room to room, turning on every light in the house until we had a bright beacon on the hill.

"Come on, everybody," I said, "we're going to have hot chocolate with marshmallows."

Dillon and Jennifer followed me back into the kitchen, and I put a kettle on to get some water boiling. Dillon opened the lower cabinet by himself and pulled out both the hot chocolate envelopes and the bag of marshmallows. I leaned up against the counter waiting for the water to boil. Jennifer found the piece of rope they used to play with the cats and began leading Snow Ball and Tiger Cat in a string tag game around the kitchen floor. She seemed happy and no longer frightened.

"Jennifer," I asked her, "did Clark say anything at all about where he was going when he left here today?"

She looked up at me and tried to remember. "I don't think so," she said. "I know he didn't think he'd be gone long."

"What did he talk about? Did he have any trouble with his truck he had to get fixed? Did he want you to wait here?"

Jennifer looked puzzled and sat down on a kitchen chair, the rope dangling loosely beside her. Both cats tried to grab it now at the same time. Jennifer looked down as they pulled in different directions. She pointed to Snow Ball.

"I heard Clark talking about Snow Ball. He said something about Snow Ball."

"Why would he talk about Snow Ball?" I said as much to myself as to Jennifer.

"He was talking to himself. He said once, 'only Snow Ball would have that.' I asked him what Snow Ball would have. He laughed and said he'd tell me after he talked to someone. That was all Clark said, Jay."

The kettle started to hum with the heating water.

"Clark is always very quiet," Jennifer said. "He doesn't talk very much."

Perceptive little kid, I thought.

"Yeah," I said, "I wish he'd tell us more than he does. But I know he loves you and Dillon just as much as I do. And I can't figure why he'd go off and leave you guys without telling you when he'd be back."

I took the kettle off and poured hot water over the marshmallows and hot chocolate Jennifer had put into cups. We carried them into the living room and took a minute to get the fireplace going. Jennifer struck the match and did the lighting.

"You want to see something funny, Jay?" she said.

"What's that?" She and Dillon seemed to be all settled down now, and Dillon was sitting in an armchair with his hot chocolate carefully held in his lap, a spoon to lap up the chocolate, and his little legs sticking straight out from the seat. Jennifer walked over to the projector, which was still set up against one side of the room. Blankets still covered the windows except for the one I'd taken down after the film showing.

"Help me rewind this film," Jennifer said. "Frederik only showed me how to run it. I don't know how to rewind."

I looked at the film. It was the first B camera reel. The one we hadn't looked at a second time. The first showing had been interrupted by Murph and Frederik knocking over the projector.

"Did you already watch this reel, Jennifer?"

She looked at me like I was being ridiculous. "Of course," she said. "I saw it this afternoon after Clark left and we had nothing to do. I put it on like Frederik showed me. Dillon saw it too."

I showed her how and she rewound the film halfway. Then she strung it through and turned it on. She set it up near the middle of the reel. Then she asked me to turn off the lights and she started the projector.

Josh was seen from across the table. The shot was made between Joan and Murph. The camera panned down. Joan and Murph were holding hands. Joan suddenly withdrew her hand. Murph went after it and grabbed it. Joan struggled to pull it out. She got it away into her lap, out of sight. Murph's hand went into her lap. It stayed there too long and then came out firmly grasping Joan's hand.

Jennifer laughed. "Wasn't that funny? Mom and Murph had a hand fight under the table. It was a secret. No one knew."

Dillon laughed with her. "A bad hand and a good hand," he said.

I turned off the projector but I didn't reach for the lights. I didn't want Jennifer or Dillon to see the expression on my face. I don't think I would have liked to see it myself. The fire flickered and reflected off the couch and armchairs. I stood up and went out into the kitchen with my empty hot chocolate cup. Jennifer followed me.

"What's the matter, Jay?" she asked.

With difficulty I smiled at her. "Nothing, sweetheart," I said, "I'm just worried about Clark."

But the film had set off a thought too. So Murph and Joan were holding hands where they thought no one could see them. But it had been picked up by the camera crew as part of the B footage. It appeared that Murph had forgotten there was a camera behind them that might pick up what was going on beneath the table. At any other dinner party, Murph and Joan wouldn't have been caught.

Murph had stopped us from seeing their slip by stepping into the picture and then pushing over the projector. That son of a bitch, I thought. And we had all thought he was drunk as a skunk.

He must have sweated through the showing of the raw film Anne had sent.

Now I remembered that Murph had convinced us not to show the first B reel during our viewing of the full takes, saying that we'd seen it before.

But so what? I could understand Murph not wanting Nan to see his little infidelity. A little hanky-panky under the table with the neighbor's wife. Donald's wife. My sister-in-law.

"Shit!" I said.

"Why'd you say that, Jay? Isn't it a bad word?"

I looked around and saw Jennifer still standing there. She was looking at me. I still held my cup in front of me and she had hers. "Yes, it is," I said. "I won't say it again. Give me that cup and get Dillon's for me too," I said.

The thing that had caused me to curse was a question. How did Murph know to interrupt the B film showing? And why didn't he care about the two A reels or the second B film reel?

"Here's mine," Dillon said, running into the kitchen. As he lifted it, it tilted sideways and some left over hot chocolate spilled onto the floor.

Murph knew what was on those reels!

"Shit!" I said again.

Dillon flinched back.

"Oh, I'm sorry," I said to him, bending down to give him a big hug. "I didn't mean you. I was saying that about something else."

Dillon laughed and was all right. I grabbed a paper towel and wiped the hot chocolate off the floor.

Murph was the guy to ask. He must have seen the stolen reels before the first B reel was shown on that Saturday night in January. He'd seen the equivalent A reel and he knew that the B version showed him and Joan fooling around under the table. Then he deliberately timed it so we'd all miss the incriminating section, which he knew—probably from Joan afterward—would appear on the first B reel.

That seemed to put Murph right in with Williams. But how? Or did it? Did Murph just arrange to have the film taken to protect himself and it had nothing to do with anything else? If what I thought was true, maybe there would be something more on the rest of the first B reel.

I walked back into the living room and dimmed the lights again. Jennifer and Dillon followed behind.

"Was there anything else 'funny' on this film?" I asked Jennifer.

"No," she said.

I started the B reel again. It went along until well past the point at which Murph and Frederik had knocked out the projector. Suddenly the camera came back to Murph and Joan. Murph was caressing Joan's arm. It was a long, slow sensual caress that took several seconds. Shortly after that, the reel ran out.

If Murph had never seen the first B reel, perhaps he thought more was on it than was seen. The B reel was missing on the day after the showing and then was found two days later. Murph must have come back in the night and taken it. But how could he check it out if Nan was with him?

My head was spinning with trying to figure all this out.

The phone rang and Jennifer and I both jumped. I walked quickly into the dining room and picked it up.

"Hello, Jay," Elaine said. "Josh and I have been calling to

come over, but nobody's been home until now. We're leaving now."

"Clark's missing," I blurted out. "We don't know where he is. He drove off this afternoon and never came back."

Elaine was not easily excited. "That's Clark sometimes. He just goes off and does some acid and thinks time stands still."

"But with Dillon and Jennifer here by themselves?" I asked her.

"It's possible," she said, but she sounded less certain. "I'll be right there, Jay."

I hung up and turned to the kids. "Josh is coming over," I said. "And Elaine thinks Clark just got lost. He'll be back soon."

"Josh coming over here," Dillon shouted and started to run around the table.

"Can we go out and meet them?" Jennifer said.

I was grasping for things to do now. I couldn't sit still and wait for Elaine.

"Sure," I said. "Let's go."

We got our jackets and boots on and walked outside. I turned the porch light on for Elaine and Josh and then we walked out toward the barn. The night was clear again with lots of stars.

"Can we go out to the pond?" Jennifer said. "I remember last winter we slid on the ice when Nick took us out to the pond at night."

I smiled at her kid memory of a happy time.

"Sure," I said.

We took the dirt road around the barn that led to the pond. Once we passed behind it, the barn blocked the light from the porch and we could really see the stars.

The kids raced ahead to the edge of the pond. When I caught up with them, they were both staring up at the stars.

"Look," Dillon said pointing. "Stars!"

"I see."

"Lots of stars, Dillon," Jennifer said and she took his hand.

I looked down at them standing by the edge of the pond. There was a log floating in the water just beyond the kids. I remembered the pond had been completely clear of debris when Clark and I walked beside it the previous night. Behind me I heard a car turning into our driveway. The lights danced against the trees across the field.

"Josh!" Dillon cried. I'm sure he recognized the sound of Elaine's old Volkswagen. The kids started to run back across the field and along the dirt road around the barn.

I turned back to the pond. My heart was pounding in my throat. I moved closer to the edge. Bending down I could just reach out and touch the end of the log. It was soft. I pulled it toward me. As it moved, it rolled over. Clark's dead face stared open eyed straight up at the stars. His long hair curled across the lower part of his face.

"Oh!" I said in a long involuntary expulsion of air from my lungs as if I'd been hit terribly hard in the center of my chest. I said it three times like some middle of the night Peter and then sat down right on the wet grass by the pond.

The movement I'd caused of the body sent a ripple out across the pond that shattered the stars there into dancing, breaking points of light. I felt the wetness of the earth seeping through my Levi's where I sat and it made me feel cold.

Somewhere distant a dog barked, then stopped.

I could smell the cold and I could feel it on my lips and my hand was very cold where it had touched the water.

I suddenly felt mad, cheated, angry.

Why was Clark dead?

Could it be an accident? He stumbled and fell into the pond? It was common knowledge that Clark couldn't swim. But the pond was so shallow, he'd have to wade out to get over his head.

Maybe he went crazy and killed himself.

I remembered he had seemed very upset that afternoon after watching Josh drag that feathered object across the grass with Snow Ball chasing it. But why?

Feathered object? A winglike object. A wing, long and feathered with . . . with bald eagle feathers?

That would make Clark crazy . . . if he thought he saw Painted River's eagle wing talisman and Snow Ball hanging from it. Sure, Clark would go around mumbling to himself about Snow Ball. The events of the vision quest had dogged him most of his adult life. If he had seen an eagle wing like the one from the vision quest, he could have gone mad.

Maybe he took some acid and wandered into the pond.

Stupid gentle son of a bitch.

I had to get him out of the water. I stood up and took two steps so that I was ankle deep in the muck at the edge of the pond. It allowed me to get a hold on his coat at his shoulders so I could drag him toward shore and up enough so that just his feet were still in the water.

His head rolled funny with my dragging him and when I was finished, I reached under it just to straighten it out. My hand came away with a sticky, black substance on it. I held my hand up close to my face. I could smell the blood more than see it.

Blood.

I got sick.

I backed away from Clark. Then I looked down at myself. Blood on one hand. My Levi's were wet all down the back from sitting on the grass. Probably I was white as a sheet too.

And Clark was murdered.

I turned to walk back to the house. Elaine could help me figure this one out. She was pretty damn smart. We had to call the police and get the body out of the pond. What should we do about the children? Maybe Elaine should take them back to her house and wait there while I took care of the body.

I stopped about halfway to the barn. Then I knelt down and wiped the blood off my hand on the wet winter grass. I shook my head in disbelief and started walking rapidly back along the dirt road around the barn. As I came around the corner, a second vehicle turned into the driveway, the headlights silhouetting Elaine and the three children until it came up and stopped next to Elaine's old Volkswagen. I saw it was Murph's four-by-four pickup.

I stopped to collect my wits. As I watched, Murph was suddenly bundling the children into the cab of the pickup. He walked around to the driver's side. Elaine stood watching it all but not moving. Suddenly I knew I didn't want him driving off with my children. I started to run toward them as fast as I could.

"Wait!" I shouted at him, waving.

$\triangledown$

Chapter 19

MURPH BROUGHT HIS TRUCK to an abrupt halt and turned off the engine and the lights. He rolled his window down and smiled out at me when I came up and peered in. Elaine moved up beside me.

"God, what happened to you, Jay?" Murph asked, looking me up and down.

"I fell into the pond," I stuttered lamely looking past him at the children. I wasn't about to tell Murph about Clark's body.

"Where are you guys off to?" I asked stupidly.

Murph looked me right in the eye. "I came over because we just got a call from Clark," he said.

Murph couldn't have surprised me more if he had slapped me across the face. I stepped back involuntarily. I suppose it was dark enough out there by the cars with the outside porch light behind me so that Murph couldn't make out the expression on my face. But my movements were enough to give me away.

Fortunately Murph seemed concentrated on his own message, and I think he wasn't really tuned in to my reaction.

"His pickup broke down on a country road. He wants us to come out and help him get things back together. I said I'd pick you up and we'd get out there just as soon as we could."

"How could . . . ," I started. "The kids . . ."

157

"I was just going to drop them with Nan," he said.

"I'll stay with the children," Elaine broke in. "I thought I might go with you. But I can't really do anything. You two go on out there and help Clark."

For a moment I thought she was talking about the Clark out behind the barn floating face up in the pond. Then I realized she meant the other Clark supposedly sitting in his pickup waiting for Murph and me to arrive with help. And I could have kissed Elaine right then. What a relief that she was there and the kids wouldn't be with Nan.

"Okay," I said. I tried to think of a way to stall for time. "Let's get the kids inside first and then we can go."

Jennifer was already opening the passenger door and jumping out of the truck. Murph got out on his side as Dillon and Josh tumbled down behind Jennifer.

Something was very wrong. What was it?

All of a sudden the name Snow Man came thundering into my brain. Snow Man, Snow Man, Snow Man. Clark had said that only Snow *Man* could have the feathered thing Snow Ball had dug her claws into, and Jennifer thought he said Snow Ball. The eagle wing talisman. Painted River's eagle wing.

I peered into Murph's face, trying to imagine what it would have looked like fifteen years younger and crisscrossed with war paint. I thought back to the couple of photographs Donald had in the 1975 album, but nothing familiar came back to me. As I looked at him, I remembered part of Donald's last message. "We are trying to beat the snow, man." Had he meant "beat the Snow Man"?

Somehow I had to get Elaine off to one side to warn her. This wasn't a business anymore for me or for her—this was a problem for Bruce Scarf and Ross Harris. Murph was walking behind me as we headed for the house and I was conscious of his footsteps.

"You really took a tumble, didn't you, Jay?" Murph said.

I turned. He was pointing to my Levi's, where the back was still wet from the grass by the pond.

"You pee your pants too or something?"

I laughed uneasily. "I'll have to be more careful where I fall," I said. He laughed too. Elaine joined us but none of us sounded sincere.

I knew that Murph had killed Clark. I just hadn't figured out why.

The key that would unravel all of this was the sting operation.

I continued walking toward the house. It was all I could do to keep from twisting around to watch his every move as he followed behind.

Once in the house, there was no way I could shake him and get to Elaine alone. In fact the only way I was able to get a moment by myself was to go into the bathroom. Murph couldn't just follow me in there. I washed away the blood that hadn't come off on the grass. I saw that Elaine had left the novel she was reading on the lid of the water tank at the back of the toilet. Elaine turned down page corners to mark the spot where she left off reading. And she was an avid reader. It was a sure thing that as soon as the children were settled in bed, she would come for the book. I opened her novel to the cornered page. Taking some lipstick from the medicine cabinet, I wrote:

MURPH IS KILLER. CLARK DEAD IN POND. CALL CAROL. CALL POLICE.

I closed the book and put it back on top of the tank lid. Then I slipped the lipstick into my pocket. I flushed the toilet and left the bathroom. Murph went in behind me but Elaine was upstairs and I couldn't get to her. He was out in seconds.

I was like one of those birds miming a broken wing to lead a fox away from the nest. I just wanted Murph out of there. I was confident Elaine would discover my message and take action.

I went upstairs with Murph right behind me to the kids' room, where all three of them were getting ready for bed.

I didn't know if I'd ever see them again.

"Good night, I love you," I said to each of them and gave them a giant hug and kiss.

I gave Josh a kiss too and then told Murph I was ready to go. I didn't mention Clark by name.

Now I was following Murph. We went down the stairs through the well-lit house and out the back door. He had on a brown tweed jacket and he seemed very, very sober. Neither of us said a word as we walked across the lawn to his pickup.

"Where do we have to go?" I asked, trying to make it sound conversational.

"He's not that far. It's about twelve miles. He's stuck on a road near Monterey."

Murph backed the car up and turned down the driveway. He seemed almost as reluctant to go as I was.

He turned west and we drove along not speaking, the headlights cutting a swath through the dark night in front of the truck.

We'd gone about five miles when Murph turned off onto a side road. I said nothing and couldn't even look at him. We'd gone about a mile when we came upon Clark's old pickup parked by the side of the road. Murph pulled up behind it and stopped. He turned off the engine but left his lights on.

We sat together like old friends communing in the silence.

"That wasn't twelve miles," I said rather stupidly.

"No, it wasn't," Murph said.

"And Clark isn't waiting for us."

"No, he's not."

He turned toward me in the dark.

"I wish you hadn't found Clark's body before I took care of it," Murph said.

He was silent a moment and then went on. "Things don't always work out the way you think they're going to."

I was nodding very slightly, but a great fear was now rising in my chest.

"I loved your sister-in-law."

He could have slaughtered me with a wet feather, I was so surprised to hear him say it.

"You loved Joan?"

I could see him nod even in the darkness of the car. I

looked out again and concentrated on Clark's pickup looming in the road ahead of us. I wondered briefly if the keys
were in the ignition.

"I loved Joan," Murph repeated.

We were silent for a moment again. "I saw the film today,"
I said.

"Yes."

"The one you blocked the first time, pretending to be
drunk. You and Joan holding hands under the table and
caught by the camera. You caressing her arm later."

"Yes, that turned out to be a stupid mistake."

"You Snow Man, Murph?"

"Yes," he said, "Snow Man."

"Clark saw the eagle wing this afternoon," I said, "and
figured out Snow Man would be the only person to have that
magic talisman of Painted River's, right?"

"Yeah, right, Jay. I'm Snow Man. I *was* Snow Man. It
seems so long ago. The war in Vietnam was still going on
when I started. They trained me in undercover. I hooked up
with Painted River. He went around the country and since
he used LSD or peyote in his ceremonies, every druggie in
the country trusted him—and Snow Man by extension. I
wrapped up a lot of drug busts. No one was wise to me. I
wore the war paint to cut the possibility of being recognized
later. Finally, I wrapped up Painted River himself."

He turned to look at me. "Painted River was great. A great
man. A guru and spiritual leader. He made hundreds of people
like Donald take life more seriously. But I had to do my job."

"Was it your job to make love to the women who came to
him too?"

Now it was his turn to be surprised. "No," he said simply.
"Joan just happened."

"How did you get here as Murph?" I asked him.

"The witness protection program. I had to disappear after
Painted River's trial. My life was in danger because of other
connections I had made. New name, new hair color, new place.
And they kept me on the payroll. Little administrative tasks
until something big might come along. It's a boring story.

"Then Joan dropped right into my lap again. They bought a house here and there she was. She didn't even recognize me until I described that time in Vermont. Then we slept together again. We really turned each other on, Jay. Believe me, it was uncontrollable."

He opened his door and started to get out.

"I don't get it, Murph," I said. "So why would you kill her?"

He gave a sharp ironic laugh. "I wanted to kill Donald. I was going to put everything I wanted together in one fell swoop. Money. Lover. Real freedom. She wasn't supposed to be going back to the city with him. She went at the last moment, and I didn't know she was in the car."

"And you ran them off the road in a blinding snowstorm," I concluded for him, "and she was dead and there was nothing to do for it."

He said nothing.

"And now she's dead, Murph."

He began to sob. "I killed her," he said, his voice breaking.

I didn't know what to say, so I waited a moment and he regained control. I thought about trying to get my door open and making a break for it while he was still distraught. But I could finger the lipstick tube in my pocket and it made me feel safe. My message, my trump card. I just had to play him along long enough for Elaine to get the kids settled and find her book.

"But Murph, I know what Donald and Joan's feelings were about agent provocateurs. I know they hated FBI, CIA, or any other kind of government secret cops. Why didn't they blow the whistle on you? Why didn't they tar and feather you and send you out of Otis on a rail?"

He made a sound as if something had stuck in his throat. Then he leaned forward and reached under the seat of the truck. I was suddenly afraid of what he would bring out—a gun, a club, a knife? But it was a nearly full pint of Wild Turkey. He twisted off the cap and took a slug, and then he passed it to me. I took one too. I needed it and it felt good going down.

"Shit, Jay, Joan knew I'd been Snow Man for about seven years now. But she didn't want to tell Donald. She didn't want him to know what she had really done during his vision quest. She thought it would spoil his life-changing experience. And me here, the fucking postmaster! She thought I was a radical hiding out, not somebody from the Bureau."

He sat quiet for a moment, thinking.

"She might have let him know we had slept together. That would be separate from the past. But she kept the Snow Man secret all those years."

"And you blew it yourself," I said, following through on his explanation.

I passed him back the Wild Turkey and he took a good swallow.

"Yeah, that's right. I blew it myself. I got too smart. I misjudged it all. It happened after that stupid filming of the dinner. I'd drunk too much. Only Donald and I were left awake at the end. He liked a drink now and again himself, you know."

He passed me the bottle again and I pretended to take more than I did and passed it back.

"And you told him you were Snow Man," I said. I tried to imagine Donald, even drunk, taking that one in. Murph trying desperately to get some respect from Donald with this confession of secrecy and power. "And you told him you'd always been FBI and there was a little filming to do the next day. A film that would catch a politician with his hand in the till. Was he interested?"

Murph was nodding. "That's right," he said. He took a second slug of the Wild Turkey without having passed the bottle back to me.

"And," I went on, "he seemed to go for it. He followed through and went to Albany and did the shoot for you."

Murph continued to nod.

"But it was blown because Weitz didn't take the bribe. Then you arranged it so your buddy in Albany, this guy John Williams, entrusted the money and the tape to Donald to return to you, right?"

Murph had stopped nodding and was just looking at me now. He was no longer sharing the whiskey.

"But I know Donald. When he came back, he was both angry and happy. Angry that you had fooled him all these years and happy he had so much on you. He was probably going to tar and feather you and your whole outfit with that tape and that money.

"And then Joan knew. If Donald knew, Joan knew. No fury like . . . She no longer wanted anything to do with you. if you hadn't already told Donald you were Snow Man, she would have then."

Murph took a deep breath and seemed about to lose control again. "That's not true," he said, leaning over and shouting it right in my face, shouting so loud that he and I both could recognize it for what it was—a confirmation.

He got out and stood up and then he bent down and peered back in at me from behind his glasses. "Come on," he said. He held the bottle in his right hand. I opened the door and got out. My heart was beating rapidly and I was frightened at what might happen next.

He would do something with me. Then he would get Clark's body, and Clark and I would end up in Clark's pickup run off the road into a lake. The cold night air surrounded me and made me shudder.

We both walked toward Clark's pickup and met between the two trucks in the bright light of the headlights. I knew he wouldn't need me mobile anymore once I was in that cab.

"You said you'd get money out of this too," I said. I just had to keep him going awhile before I played my message-to-Elaine trump card. I gripped the lipstick tube to feel its smooth cover with my fingers.

He gave another of those ironic short laughs. "You're too smart, Jay. The money burned up in the crash too. Money, lover, everything gone in one deal."

"No," I said, "it's too easy. And I think I've got it. There was never $500,000 in that briefcase. You'd taken a lot of it out before the fire. Every piece of proof points to $500,000. Who's to know that it was not all there. And no one has to account for it. *You* don't have to account to your boss for it. You deliberately sent Donald back to New York to deliver the money and the tape and told him to keep it quiet. Donald consented, because he was going to blow whistles all over town."

"Fuck it, Jay. I've worked for this stupid government for seventeen years and never got paid shit and never saved a penny. My whole fucking life is a lie. And I always see these drug guys with thousands and thousands of dollars in cash that slips right through my hands.

"Who knows what happened." He stopped, waving the bottle around more to make my point for me. Then a strange sick smile crossed his lips. "At least I didn't come away with nothing."

"That's why the car burned after the accident," I went on. "It had to burn to get rid of the evidence that the cash was short and you had to start the fire. In fact, it really didn't matter if they were dead or not, as long as the car burned and no one knew you'd started the fire."

Maybe I could rattle him if I got it all right.

"And the videotape?" I asked. "Didn't you want to get the videotape away from them?"

"Aw, I looked for it," he said, "but it wasn't in the wreck." Then he stopped suddenly, recognizing that he didn't want to tell me that. "In my job I've killed several people. You just arrange it and you do it." He regained control with that horrifying admission. I knew he was saying he'd do it this one more time.

"And Nan?" I asked. "You'd kill her too?"

He suddenly swung the Wild Turkey bottle down hard against the front of his own truck. It hit the parking light under the headlight and both the bottle and the light shattered. The parking light went out. We both looked at it and the broken glass on the road. Then he laughed to regain control.

"You never heard of divorce, Jay? Come on," he said and he started down the road past Clark's truck.

"Wait," I said. I had no way of knowing if Elaine was ready, but I couldn't wait any longer. "I have to tell you something, Murph."

He turned around and looked at me. His glasses caught the lights so that I couldn't see his eyes.

"I left a message for Elaine." I took the lipstick out of my pocket and held it up. The gold tube caught in the headlights and sparkled. "I wrote it on the page she was reading in the book left in the bathroom."

"I'm disappointed in you, Jay," Murph said. He reached into his pocket and took out some folded paper. He opened it up and handed it to me. It was the two pages from Elaine's book where I had written the message. The red lipstick letters jumped out at me in the bright headlights. I let the pages flutter to the ground at my feet.

"Come on," he said.

He took me by the arm and started pulling me along down the road. I went. I had a feeling that Murph was ready for anything and nothing I could do would make any difference. When he came alongside the pickup, he opened the door and told me to get in. I put a hand up on the open door. I knew that if I got in I wouldn't be getting out. Murph was just behind me. He gripped my right arm with his left hand and had taken hold of the door frame.

But I thought of something else.

"And the kids," I said.

Murph shrugged. "I love 'em but I can't do anything about it. Like you said, they get the money left from the fire. The Bureau is never going to confess to the Weitz scam. They'd be laughed out of Washington. East West Imports, Limited, is dead-ended. Williams has disappeared. It's the kids' money now."

"Yeah, big deal, it's nothing but a big tax bill. Maybe they lose the house."

"I can't help out on that one," Murph said.

"Jennifer and Dillon are your children, Murph."

Murph pushed his face forward so that our noses were almost touching, and I could smell the whiskey on his breath when he spoke.

"What the fuck are you talking about?"

"Donald was sterile. He couldn't have children. You must be the father."

"You're lying."

"No, I'm not, Murph. Joan never told you? Did she say she was wearing a diaphragm all the times you got together? They wanted children. Maybe she just 'forgot' a few times. Maybe she only 'forgot' twice. I don't know. But I do know that Jennifer and Dillon are not Donald's children. Think about the kids and you'll know they're yours."

When he moved up into my face, I could see that I'd stunned him. He still held my right arm and was holding tightly on to the door frame with his right hand to give himself leverage to push me forward. His hand was against the door jamb of the truck itself, where the open door would close on it. This was the only time I would get him by surprise. I tightened my grip where I braced myself against the open door.

"What color hair did you have Murph, as Snow Man? What color before you dyed it? Before your disguise?" I asked.

"Believe me, Murph," I said almost in a shout, moving forward very slightly as if to make my point and clearing myself of the door. "It's the God's truth."

And in the same moment I said it, I slammed the door hard.

I saw him form the word "red" with his lips. And I could see in his eyes he knew it was the truth.

The door caught the fingers of his right hand hard, smashing against the knuckles, then bounced open. Murph doubled over in surprise and pain. I took off running down the road out of the lights. I had gone about fifty feet when a shot rang out behind me.

Shit, he did have a gun.

I vaulted over a ditch and felt something give along the muscles of my knife wound. I ran deep into the woods and then collapsed on the ground clutching at my leg, and panting heavily.

I looked back and listened while Murph turned the pickup

around so that the headlights lit up the road in the direction I had gone. Then he turned off the engine again. For about three minutes everything was quiet and I began to get my breath back. Then I heard Murph calling me from the road.

"Jay," he shouted. "It's okay, Jay. I didn't know they were mine." He waited for my reply. "Believe me, I didn't know. I won't do anything more to hurt them."

Quiet.

"Come on, Jay. I'll drive you home." I heard him rustling in the bushes along the road on the same side I was on. But I didn't move and I didn't believe he would find me.

"Jay," he shouted, "I'm going to wait in the car. Let's go home."

I was able to make him out walking back along the road to his pickup. He got in and then the lights went out.

The back of my Levi's were still wet from where I had sat by the pond. My feet were wet from the pond. The night got colder and I found myself trembling with fear. We waited each other out for an hour.

Then I won. The engine started and he drove away.

Chapter 20

I STOOD UP AND tried to walk to the road. My leg hurt but I didn't think anything of it. I took several steps before I collapsed on the ground holding on to my thigh. After several minutes the pain subsided. But Murph had neutralized me successfully. I wasn't going very far. For about fifteen minutes I just sat there trying to get comfortable with the cold and the pain in my leg. I began to wish I hadn't told him the children were his. What he would do now was beyond my control. I couldn't walk and I couldn't get anywhere to warn Elaine or the children or call Carol. They were all on their own.

I began to crawl through the woods toward the road, where I could signal the first passing car in the morning. I knew the road was too little used to expect anyone before the local farmers got up at dawn. I had crawled about twenty feet, dragging the leg painfully along, when I came to a fallen branch that was just the right size for a crutch. With it, I was able to raise myself up and limp toward the road.

When I was nearly there, I looked carefully both ways as if I were a child just learning to cross. Except I was looking for a murderer. I nearly jumped out of my pants when I saw the glimmer of light from the stars reflect something down the road to my right.

Clark's pickup!

I was so frightened by Murph and distracted by pain that
I hadn't thought of the pickup. Maybe Murph had forgotten
it too.

Using my improvised crutch, I came out of the bushes and
made my way carefully along the road. I stayed close enough
to cover that I could disappear quickly into the brush.

I finally reached the truck, its door still open. I came alongside and pulled myself up into the seat behind the wheel.
Then I reached for the ignition.

There was no key there.

I was stuck out here in the dark.

Clark's truck had a cab plus a jump seat behind the front
seat. I knew he kept an old sleeping bag there for emergen-
cies. Luckily, the bag lay right on top of his tools and the
other stuff and I pulled it out. With the door closed and the
sleeping bag wrapped around me, I became a lot warmer and
stopped shuddering.

I didn't fall asleep, but I wasn't quite awake either when
I heard the sound of a vehicle coming down the road. I had
opened the door and was preparing to get out to wave it down
but some animal sense held me back. Then the vehicle came
around the bend.

I could see the smashed left front parking light was out.
Murph was coming back.

I left the door open. It was how he would expect it if he
remembered how he left it. But I couldn't run for it. I pulled
myself over the seat into the storage space behind it and
covered my body with the old sleeping bag. I started shaking
again and couldn't stop.

Murph's truck came alongside and stopped. First one door
opened and slammed, and then the other one. Then I heard
the tailgate open. I took the sleeping bag off my face and I
could see the beam of a flashlight bobbing around.

"This son of a bitch is just too big," I heard Murph say.
Something fell heavily to the ground off his pickup.

"I don't want to take him," a woman's voice said. I recognized Nan.

"Come on," Murph said, "we've been over that enough

times. He's only two years old. He's not going to remember."

Two years old! They were talking about taking Dillon with them. They were talking about kidnapping.

They were dragging something my way. I heard the open door creak as it was pulled open farther.

"I wish he hadn't smashed this damn hand on me," Murph said. "This guy weighs a fucking ton."

"He's had enough trouble," Nan said. "Leave him with his family."

Murph gave a grunt. Something made the truck rock as the weight caught the edge of it.

"I *am* his family!" Murph said.

I heard Nan give out with a sound that was part sigh, but I think she was turned toward me and away from him and I'd swear she said, "I'm not."

I wondered if he was right. If he was Dillon's father, maybe he could take him. Would a judge let a father like Murph take a kid? But no one was asking a judge. He was going to take Dillon anyway.

I peeked out just in time to see a head loom over the back seat as it came up into the cab. I ducked down quickly. It was Clark—they were putting the body into the truck.

Murph gave another grunt and I could feel the body slide across the seat in front of me. Murph climbed up into the cab beside it. All he had to do was to look behind the seat and pull the sleeping bag off me.

"Besides, he's just going to sleep until morning. Nobody's going to be able to follow us after that."

"This isn't going to work, Frank," Nan said.

"Shut up," Murph told her shortly. He huffed and puffed for a moment, then I heard the sound of the key fitting into the ignition.

"I'll follow you," he said to Nan. "And be careful not to wake the kid."

I heard her walking away from the truck. They must have Dillon asleep in their truck.

"Dumb woman," Murph said under his breath. "He *is* my kid!"

He started the truck and the engine roared to life. In a moment, the truck was moving. I lay as still as I could, glad the truck was going so that my own quaking didn't shake it. I couldn't judge the time very well, but it must have been close to twenty minutes before Murph brought Clark's truck to a stop. He turned off the engine and the lights. He opened the door and got out, but then started moving Clark's body again. This time it seemed he was just shifting it around. He groaned and grunted a lot and then seemed satisfied with whatever he had done. I heard him get out and walk away, and I sat up cautiously and peered out. Murph and Nan were standing by the other truck about one hundred feet ahead of Clark's. Nan had left the Ford's lights on. I could see the bridge in front of their truck—I also remembered the steep incline that ran down to the right of the bridge, ending in a little picnic ground beyond which there was a forty-foot drop to a deep pool in the river below.

Clark's head was hunched over the wheel as if he were asleep. Murph had thrust one of his arms through the steering wheel to brace it and give the truck direction in its final path.

Nan had walked back so that the two of them were between the trucks and nearer to theirs than Clark's. This was my only shot.

I sat up and grabbed Clark by the ponytail, pulling him back hard. He came back so that his arms came free and his head went back over the seat and turned sideways. He was looking right at me. First, I checked to make sure Murph had left the keys in the ignition. They were there. Then I leaned past Clark and turned on the lights.

Murph and Nan both looked back at the Dodge curiously. I reached past Clark, opened the door, and pushed hard. I looked up again as Clark's body tumbled to the pavement. The opening door and the motion of Clark's body must have scared the hell out of them. I'm sure they thought he was still alive. Then Murph started to move toward me. I reached down and turned the key in the ignition. The engine growled once, but didn't catch. Murph was running. I tried again and the engine came to life. I waited for Murph. He had pulled a gun out and was waving it in his good hand as he ran. I knew he couldn't see beyond the lights. I gunned the engine. Murph leapt out of the way as I bore down on him.

Then there was just Nan. She began to run toward the Ford, but she had waited too long. Murph was behind me shouting something. Nan had come alongside their truck, and I had to slow down so that I wouldn't pitch Dillon through the windshield or something if he was asleep on the front seat. I probably nudged the back of the truck at under ten miles an hour. But it was an impact, and it shoved it away from Nan just as she reached for the door. Then I stepped on the gas again and the Dodge caught on the bumper of the Ford and pushed it, causing it to veer to the right without a driver.

I saw Nan looking up at me as I passed her. Her lips were moving in a peculiar way, but no sound was coming out of her mouth. I sped up but it seemed the Ford might miss the concrete guardrail on the bridge and veer completely off through a wire cable and into the water below. I backed off and it changed direction and caught along the concrete. I came back and took it slowly again and sped up as the sparks flew from the right front fender acting as a guide along the guardrail. The back of the Ford was packed with everything Nan and Murph owned that they could fit in. I saw a small face peering out of the rear window at me.

"Hang on, Dillon," I shouted. "Hang on just another minute more."

I wished he could hear me. We moved along the bridge like that, bouncing on and off the retaining rail for another fifty feet before the Ford's steering made it go out into a spin, so that it came to a stop facing the other direction. I stopped alongside it.

Dillon looked at me through the window. I put the Dodge in neutral and pulled on the hand brake. Then I jumped out. Of course, I fell flat on my face. I'd forgotten that one leg wouldn't work. I pulled myself up using the side of the truck to brace myself and opened the door. Dillon tumbled down into my arms. He started to cry hysterically.

"It's okay," I said. "It's going to be okay now."

But I looked back down the road. Murph was back there about just reaching the bridge, running hard. I shoved off against Murph's truck and managed to reach the Dodge. Then I pushed Dillon into the cab ahead of me and climbed in over him. I heard Murph coming up on the driver's side. I heard him panting heavily, winded. He banged on my window with his gun as he stepped up on the running board. But I put the pickup in gear, let off the brake, and gunned the engine. He couldn't hang on with his smashed fingers and hold the gun too. He fell away from the window. I heard a shot from behind us as we moved away, and something pinged off the roof at the same time.

Then we were gone.

Dillon cried for about five more minutes before he finally snuggled up against me and went to sleep. When we came up the driveway to the house, we saw lights in every room. And a state trooper's car was parked outside.

"What happened, Jay?" Elaine shouted as she ran to meet me. I opened my door and pointed to the sleeping Dillon.

"Help me out and I'll tell you," I said.

She took Dillon and the trooper helped me get into the house. I let the trooper know where to find Murph and Nan and Clark's body. He went out to his car to call in somebody to the site.

While I told Elaine the whole story, she took me in beside the fire with a dry blanket and got me the bottle of Scotch, making sure I took a couple of good belts from it.

"What happened here?" I asked her as soon as I had control of myself. "How did they get Dillon?"

Elaine shrugged. "First of all, somebody ripped out two pages of the book I was reading."

"Yeah, Murph," I told her. "It was a message I'd left you in lipstick. He took it out so you wouldn't get it."

"That made me angry. I thought something really weird must be happening.

"Then Murph and Nan came back here. They went

straight past the house and out behind the barn. I thought
it was you and Murph—maybe Clark too. But in about fifteen minutes Nan came walking up to the house. I asked
Nan what Murph was doing and where you were. She said
you were with Clark and Murph had just come back to get
a tire Clark had left behind the barn.

"She looked a mess, Jay. Her hair was all screwed up and
I could tell she'd been crying.

"I asked her what was wrong—why she was so upset."

Elaine shook her head and bit her lip. Then she went on.
"She said she didn't want to talk about it. Then she did
something so out of character that I knew she was really on
the edge—she asked for some of that Scotch, almost pleading
with me. So I got the bottle out and poured her a stiff double
shot. She downed it as if she'd been doing it all her life. Then
she just sat there, staring straight ahead.

"I sat here with her. Murph came up with the truck and
came inside. He said he needed to get something out of
Clark's room upstairs. I was edgy but there was no way I'd
have guessed he was getting Dillon. I didn't follow him
around the house. I just sat here with Nan. I know he came
back down and went out carrying something. Honest, Jay, I
didn't know it was Dillon. He probably slept right through
almost all of it.

"A moment later there was a light tap on a horn outside, and
we both looked and saw Murph waving to Nan to come on."

Elaine was shaking her head thoughtfully.

"Then she said something that shook me up. 'Take the
kids away from here now,' she said, 'and don't bring 'em back
until it's safe.'

"I asked her what she was talking about. But she just
shook her head. 'Don't bring 'em back until Jay's here. It'll
be safe then.'

"She turned and went out the door so quickly that I didn't
have a chance to question her."

Elaine turned and looked at the trooper, who had come
back in. "Even then, if it hadn't been for the pages ripped
out of the book, I don't think I would have done anything.

That was the tipoff, Jay. Only you could have had something to do with that.

"I went to get the children. Dillon was gone. I feel sure that Nan didn't know Murph had already taken him. Two minutes later I was on the phone to the cops."

"I love you, Elaine," I said. "You're really something."

The trooper smiled.

Then Jennifer came down the stairs.

"What's going on?" she said.

"Lots of excitement," Elaine said. "We will tell you all about it in the morning."

"Just give me a hug," I said.

Jennifer came up and put her little arms around me. Then she turned up her nose and backed off. "Golly, Jay, you smell awful."

Elaine and I smiled, and Jennifer went running off to bed.

It was another half hour before a Connecticut State Police car arrived and I was looking into the tired eyes of Sergeant Ross Harris. The children were all asleep. And by then the police had found Clark's body on the road. But the banged-up Ford pickup and Murph and Nan were gone.

Later, when I had warmed up and even though I felt like a Mexican piñata after a birthday party, Ross helped me out to his car and we drove across the street. He helped me hobble up the steps to Murph and Nan's house. Ross kept shaking his head, saying "I dunna feel good about this."

They had left the furnishings all in place but the closets were empty. And there was no sign of an eagle wing talisman. Murph couldn't give it up.

The Ford pickup was found twenty-four hours later down a farm lane, empty. Even all the stuff I'd seen packed into the back was gone.

Three days later I received a letter from Murph. Well, not a letter, a notarized statement and not exactly from Murph, but I knew the source. It arrived at the office in New York

City and had been mailed in Albany. The notarized statement said that East West Imports, Limited, of the Grand Cayman Islands had repaid a debt of $500,000 to Donald Jasen. The repayment had been made on December 27 in cash. The statement said Donald and Joan had loaned the company the money over the course of the past ten years and it gave dates and amounts of the loans. The total loan had been $340,000 and this was the repayment of that principal and $160,000 interest.

I looked up from the statement, my eyes nearly glazing over with the memories. The son of a bitch had tried to kill me and kidnap my kid. Now he was handing me a way out of the tax thing. Murph had been listening when I'd talked about taxes. And he did believe the kids were his.

But Murph had been right—no one was stepping forward to claim the salvaged money. It was Donald's. There was nothing but my word to indicate the briefcase contained something less than $500,000 in the first place. The only tangible evidence anyone had was the receipt from East West Imports, Limited, for $500,000 and a notarized statement from the same company, for the same amount.

Carol and I worked out the numbers for the kids using the East West Imports statement. There was now only $160,000 in taxable income of the $500,000. That was the interest. The result was that the kids now came up with a little over $75,000 they could bank from the $500,000 instead of losing everything they owned. I'd run it by Jerry Barnes as soon as I could, but the only way the IRS was going to prove they owed more was by getting evidence that the money was something other than a loan repayment. Which was okay with me too. They'd have to get straight to Williams and Murphy, or whatever his new name was. Catch them if they can.

Scarf called two weeks later—while Carol and I were still scrambling to catch up on our tax season load. I had a client sitting in front of me at the time, a fussy woman who looked at her watch when I took Scarf's call to be sure I wouldn't

charge her for the time I was taking away from our appointment.

"What's happening, my man?" Scarf said.

"How you feeling, Bruce?" I retorted.

"It's about your old friend. You remember Murph, don't
you?"

My heart skipped a beat. "You find him?" I said.

"Nope," he said.

I didn't know whether to laugh or cry.

"In fact," Bruce went on, "the man don't look like he ever
existed."

"That a fact," I said. "He seemed pretty solid to me."

Bruce chuckled. "I wish I could tell you. But it's like running down the wind or something. Just when you think you
got it, it's gone again."

"His friends take care of him?" I asked. The woman in
front of me raised an eyebrow and pointed to her watch.

"I can't even get that far. But I think so. Either that or he
set up his own program this time. But he didn't have enough
bread to do that, did he?"

"I don't know, Bruce," I said. "He might have. He might
have."

"Also, Ross Harris got a specialist to look at X rays of
Donald's multiple concussions. A new conclusion: caused
by several blows with a flat, blunt instrument, not the rolling
convertible."

"So it's certain, Donald was murdered?"

"You got it," Bruce said.

"You figure out why they went after the congressman?"

Bruce was quiet for a moment. He seemed to speak reluctantly. "I know some of those boys," he said. "They stood
back while we used to beat up the kids in the old days. Seems
Weitz is out to put some reins back on the Bureau. These
boys been on the run ever since the old man died. Seems
they thought they could dirty up Weitz by throwing the green
at him." Bruce's deep laugh came at me. "Man, they messed
that one up."

I signed off just as my client started clicking her tongue. But

I wondered if someday I would buy a country house and take some letters to a local post office and be looking at an aging Murph. He would look me up and down from behind a different style of glasses and with a different hair color, but I would know him in a second and start shaking all over again.

In June, I got a call that contained another surprise. It was a Saturday morning and I was ready to go out.

"Hello, Mr. Jasen."

It was the kind of voice I knew could drive me crazy and I knew I'd heard it before.

"Yes," I said guardedly. I was prepared to turn down a tax return just based on the voice.

"This is Ben Withers here. You remember me, don't you?"

I have to admit, he made me smile.

"Sure, Ben," I said, "how could I forget?"

"How's my cats?"

"They're just fine. Believe me, they've gotten into all kinds of trouble."

Old Ben chuckled. "And the missus?"

Carol was sitting at her desk, the French doors were open. I glanced across at her. She was looking puzzled.

"The missus is fine too, Ben," I said. Carol understood and smiled. "And your missus?"

He chuckled a little again. "Getting ready to serve up a mess of strawberries at the Methodist church tomorrow night. It's our strawberry festival. You should come up and bring the kiddies."

"Sounds like fun," I said, but I couldn't believe it was the reason he called. At least it wasn't tax season, and I was prepared to wait him out.

"Well," he said.

I waited.

"I was just a little curious as to what was on that videotape your brother lost up here."

I took a deep breath and then I told him. I told Ben the whole story from beginning to end. The only thing I left out was the part about Murph being the father. I told him about the accident and about the film and about the dinners to watch the films in the country. I told him about the vision quest and I told him about Snow Man and how the name was similar to Snow Ball. I told him about the eagle wing talisman. I told him about Clark being dead in the pond and I told him about my drive with Murph. And I told him about Murph and Nan disappearing without a trace. Farmer Withers got the earful of his life. At the end it seemed as if he would double over with pleasure.

"That sure is the best gol-darned story I think I've ever heard," he said. "Wait till I tell my son-in-law."

"Feel free," I said.

"He's the one first saw the wreck burning, you know," Farmer Withers said.

"What?" I said.

"Yeah, he came up on it just after midnight. He saw the man trying to throw snow on the fire."

"Man trying to throw snow on the fire?" I repeated after him dumbly.

"Yes, indeed, there was a man—he was a bald fellow—trying to put the fire out by throwing snow on it. My son-in-law shouted to him that he was going for help. He's the one called the fire department."

"A bald man was throwing snow on the fire?" I said. "And it was after midnight?"

"Yep."

"Did he tell the police about that?"

"Nope."

I was very quiet on my end of the phone.

"Should he have? He said they'd already heard about the fire when he called in. He figured the bald fella reported it."

I still couldn't find a word to say.

"Well I got to get down to the barn and set up a new milking machine. Hope we see you up in these parts sometime soon. And don't forget to give my regards to the missus."

He had hung up on me. I couldn't believe it, but Mr. Withers who you couldn't get off the phone on a bet had hung up on me. I quickly looked up his number and called him back. The line was busy. I was certain it was going to be busy for days while he got the story out.

But what he had said was that my brother was alive after midnight. Murph must have had to go back and finish the job, which explained the findings of Harris's expert. The children would have a lot of money. The casualty loss could now be included in the same year Donald died. Included on their final return.

Now Jennifer and Dillon had the $147,000 saved from the fire and another $46,000 from tax refunds from Donald and Joan's current tax return and the refund from carrying back the loss to their return of three years ago. In short, the children had over $193,000 in the bank.

I turned to Carol who was staring at me, waiting. I shook my head in disbelief.

"There's good news and there's bad news," I said.

Jennifer appeared around the corner with little Dillon in tow.

"No joking with Carol now," she said. "You promised we'd leave for the zoo five minutes ago. If you were still our uncle, we'd be there already."

I put on a long face and Dillon laughed.

"It's okay," Jennifer said. "I like you being our dad."